The
ILLUMINATION
of
ALICE MALLORY

60 YEARS IN CANADA
19 33
19 93
HarperCollins

The
ILLUMINATION
of
ALICE MALLORY

MAUREEN MOORE

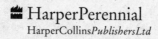
HarperPerennial
HarperCollinsPublishersLtd

The author gratefully acknowledges the Canada Council/le Conseil des Arts du Canada for awarding her a project grant to aid in the writing of this novel.

For the use of extracts from the writings of D. H. Lawrence the publisher wishes to acknowledge the Estate of Frieda Lawrence Ravagli.

The author asserts the moral right to be identified as the author of this work.

First published in 1991 by HarperCollins Publishers Ltd, London

First HarperPerennial edition: 1993

Canadian Cataloguing in Publication Data

Moore, Maureen, 1943-
The illumination of Alice Mallory

1st HarperPerennial ed.
ISBN 0-00-647493-4

I. Title.

PS8576.0486I54 1993   C813'.54   C92-095787-0
PR9199.3.M622I54 1993

93 94 95 96 97 98 99 CW 10 9 8 7 6 5 4 3 2 1

For
ROBERTA SONOLET

CHAPTER ONE

NORTH VANCOUVER was utterly loathsome and desolate, Alice Mallory decided, especially lower Lonsdale where she lived. Lonsdale Avenue was North Vancouver's main street and although it began as a pleasant boulevard on the crest of a hill it ended at the bottom of the incline as a patched, dingy street flanked by small, dark stores. North Vancouver had as much splendour and mystery as a parking lot. It was not Europe. It was not literature. From reading novels she knew it was not even Real Life.

Despite this, her mother, Beryl, actually liked North Vancouver and got on well with Maggie who owned the second-hand furniture store on Lonsdale where the two women sat smoking and drinking tea in the afternoons. Alice was certain her mother would never move to a more interesting location. Inevitable morning drizzle began to fall as Alice waited for the bus that would carry her over the Lions Gate Bridge to her job at Woolworth's, but in her imagination she was in a brilliant Paris café where she pushed her dark hair back carelessly, caught up in exalted conversation. Now she clasped a D. H. Lawrence novel as if it were a sacred text; she didn't want to see herself creeping down Lonsdale in some geriatric future, clanking a walker in front of her thin, old lady's legs and yet how could she avoid this fate? She was not blonde. Men did not faint at the sight of her. Interesting strangers did not seek her out.

On the bus, passengers stared straight ahead like prisoners and water ran down the windows as the vehicle accelerated along Marine Drive. Alice had often listened to Beryl and Maggie discussing the rich, clear pattern of male guilt that ran through the lives of women. 'I went through hell,' Beryl would proclaim in a harsh, nasal voice, describing the wartime pregnancy that had culminated in the birth of her daughter, Alice. Eyes blazing, Beryl would grab a listener's arm. In fact, Alice noticed, her mother's hands were always gripping something; a cup, the arm of a chair, and, in photographs, a man. 'I had no one,' Beryl would cry in bitter reminiscence. 'Her father, that creep, was off in the effing army.'

Alice's brother, David, was finally in school and Beryl was recovering from years of waiting for the custodial care of the public education system. The member of the household who caused her the least inconvenience was David's father, Mr Goldman. At Maggie's, Beryl recounted domestic sorrows while she hunched over her cup of tea and cigarette, as if fearing someone might snatch these comforts away.

Alice admired efficient vivacity and was vigilant against bouts of melancholy that descended upon her like a malaise for which literature was the only cure. The fifties were almost over and she saw herself in a radiant, new era where she'd be borne up by art, lifted away from the heavy downward pull she could feel dragging at her. It was possible, through sternness and will, to change her nature, to become more like the people in Lawrence's book, to be definite and certain, invincible with opinion. Wendy Gregg, the clerk on Woolworth's cosmetic counter, was this sort of person. Her eyelids were streaked with blue and she'd chased her older brother with a broom and had broken the handle over his back.

'Why?'

'He bugged me.'

She was Alice's ideal. Her order sheets were always neatly filled out and handed in on time. The displays on her counter were never allowed to empty.

At Woolworth's, Alice donned one of the nylon smocks clerks wore over their clothes. 'Can I serve you?' was the humiliating query emblazoned on it in red zigzag stitching.

Lawrence described a family in which a precise, spirited mother buoyed her children up so they would not descend into a life of brutish toil. On her lunch hour Alice turned the pages of this novel in a passionate swoon, reading about a woman who recognized that her son, Paul, was an artist whose soul was gripped by ecstatic perceptions and insights. Afterwards, Alice reorganized the rainwear display, bracing her back against a post and heaving rubbery garments on to hooks. She comforted herself by remembering she still had another break, dividing her day into portions of bearable time punctuated by consoling intervals.

'Jeez, you've always got some book in your hand,' Doris commented in the staffroom later. She was a small, quick woman who'd worked on the pet counter for fifteen years and her arms were perfectly smooth due to her habit of torching off any fuzz with a cone of burning paper.

Alice looked up from her novel in a daze, her eyes as dark as those of someone drugged.

'What are you reading?' Doris persisted.

'*Sons and Lovers*,' Alice answered, holding up the library book with its plain, solemn cover.

'What's that when it's at home?' Doris screeched. 'I don't even want to think about it. Did you hear that, Carol?'

The head girl stared at her freshly painted red fingernails. 'Sick,' she commented in a bored voice, waving her hands to dry the bright coating. There was a long, high window on one side of the room through which the women could glimpse an oblong of sky, and by the end of the day the air in the staffroom was sharp with accumulated cigarette smoke and the odour of discarded crusts and lunchbags.

'Oh, leave her alone.' Wendy spun around from her place at the mirror. The women applied cosmetics in a little flurry just before the end of their breaks, sitting at the mirror provided by the management for that purpose.

Alice avoided this mirror, considering her face to be totally unmodern and out of style, with dark brown eyes instead of riveting blue ones and an absence of other desirable qualities, such as savage cheekbones and flaxen curls. She had a pale face she judged barely acceptable, but her nose was not pert and her eyebrows were far too thick. Tugging at a tendril of hair she returned to her book. If she couldn't look stunningly dramatic, she wished she at least appeared normal. People often gazed at her consideringly, asking where she was from, and when she was younger she'd imagined absurdly that she was Mr Goldman's child too (though that was clearly impossible), her black hair mirroring the previous shade of his, now evident only in old photographs.

Wendy rose from her chair and the others followed her through the dark hall, thrusting their timecards into the machine and trooping past the office where Brenda took their purses through a slot in the window. As she trailed after the others, clattering down the wooden steps to the main floor, Alice tried not to think of the fact that this was her last break. About now, her mother would glance at the clock on the wall of Maggie's store and stub out her cigarette in the brass ashtray with a smoking dog on it, pushing herself up reluctantly. Alice had viewed this ritual many times on her days off.

'Time to put the potatoes on,' Beryl would announce.

'I'll see you soon then,' Maggie would answer in her slow, fatigued voice.

'Matches, keys,' Beryl would mutter, her lank brown hair falling into her eyes. Alice thought she'd go mad when she pictured it. Her mother's rubber thongs would slap along the sidewalk as she marched home. Beryl was full of theories about the value of rubber footwear in Vancouver's wet climate. Once in the kitchen, Beryl would survey the filthy breakfast dishes and gaze at sour pots on the stove, still soaking from the day before. A rag of curtain hung over the small window above the sink where she could peer out into the tangle of back yard.

In the cold living room, David would lie immobilized in front of the television, his eyes dark under a thick fringe of brown hair, his mouth open while he watched three men leaping about on the screen, smacking each other on the head. Mr Goldman, a small man with a noble, semitic profile and beautiful hands, would be sitting in his laundromat, surrounded by washers and driers whirling the clothing of strangers. After locking up, he'd make his way to Beryl's, just as he did every evening.

On the bus that took her back over the arc of steel and concrete suspended over Burrard Inlet, Alice gazed down at water where tugs pulled barges and small craft sped through waves, trailing threads of foam. I'm almost twenty, she thought, rubbing at the glass, helpless with yearning. After she finished the supper dishes she heard Mr Goldman's key in the lock and dropped her wet dishtowel on the counter. Gazing through the doorway between the kitchen and living room she tried to avoid seeing the old couch with its salmony bedspread and the two upholstered chairs angled towards the flickering grey eye of the television. The carpet was soiled and the surrounding wood floor, greyish, flecked with occasional slivers of golden wax applied long ago by some former occupant. Above, pale, wavery blossoms of damp stained the ceiling.

Mr Goldman entered wearily. In high school he'd won an academic medal and Beryl said his hair was thin because he'd tugged it in fits of nervous, ambitious study. He laid his folded newspaper on the little table beside his chair while David, already dressed in blue polo pyjamas, scrambled on to his knee. The child leaned ecstatically against his father's chest, watching as Mr Goldman pulled a cigar from his pocket and drew off the fragrant, golden paper that encircled it. Slipping the gleaming, fragile ring on to his grubby thumb, the boy held his hand out for Beryl and Alice to admire.

Beryl looked up from her programme. On the screen a woman was weeping because she'd won a set of Danish modern bedroom furniture. 'Bed,' Beryl commanded, turning her eyes back to the television.

Mr Goldman set David down and watched his son's small figure walk through the arched doorway into the hall leading to his bedroom. Then he unfolded his paper and took out his fountain pen to do the crossword puzzle. Alice planned to wander into his laundromat one day and begin a conversation in which all the unsaid speeches she had made to him in her imagination would be uttered. When she was a child, Mr Goldman had taken her out in a rowboat on Lost Lagoon, removing his jacket and stepping into the quivering craft, even though Beryl had blown smoke out of her nostrils and complained the adventure was a waste of money. Afraid of water, Beryl had paced along the shore, while Alice and Mr Goldman

· 11 ·

circumnavigated the fountain, and swans dipped fluid necks into the glistening water. The sun glittered and reflected light shone on to Mr Goldman's face.

'How was work today?' Mr Goldman asked Alice now. She admired his voice with its European accents and guttural consonants. If only she could reply to this kind of question deeply and fully, the way people did in novels.

'Don't ask me how *my* day was!' Beryl burst out. 'I'm alone all day in this dump!'

She gestured at the dingy walls that could never be repainted because they belonged to the landlord. Beryl's nerves were bad, firing messages in response to the menace and treachery of the world. The woman at the Salvation Army store overcharged her and the cashier at the supermarket short-changed her. Clerks schemed to sell her defective merchandise.

She told the household about it at night. 'So this jerk said to me . . . I told him . . . ' Her face would be screwed up with resentment. 'They can't put one over on me,' she exclaimed after one of her shopping trips. 'How do you think those bastards get rich while we stay poor! You have to be on your toes. Are you listening?'

Mr Goldman would sigh, 'Don't let it get you so upset, Beryl. Don't let it get you down.'

The boy at the supermarket had it in for her, Alice's mother would inform her listeners.

Life was a battle. Beryl wore a tight, padded brassiere under her matted sweater, the underwear sewn in hard, concentric circles, like the breastplates of female warriors. Around her hips she zipped a thick fitted skirt she'd bought from the Sally Ann. Thus girded, fortified with tea and cigarettes, she'd venture on to Lonsdale, lingering by the shop windows. At the butcher shop she would peer suspiciously through the glass, since butchers had been known to mix bread into the meat they ground. They hid lumps of fat underneath the lean.

'Nobody gives a shit about me,' Beryl continued. She'd painted a scarlet mouth over her own pale, pinched one.

Mr Goldman sat in a pool of light from the lamp. 'Now, Beryl.'

'Don't "now Beryl" me. I've got a splitting headache. Does anybody ask? David comes home and it's TV, TV, TV. Then the Big Girl comes home and it's read, read, read.' Beryl chewed at her bright bottom lip, staining her front teeth red. 'I might as well be alone here. Now you're doing the crossword puzzle!'

Alice got up and crept down the hallway with her book. It was ironic her mother had met Mr Goldman at a dance where she'd been in her element and hadn't realized that quiet, reserved Mr Goldman had never been to a dance before. Beryl claimed she was impressed he'd worn a suit.

'You know what I mean? He wasn't fresh like the other guys. He had class.'

'Did you know you'd fall in love?'

'Love! Oohing and aahing. What's important is that the guy contributes. Not like your father. He never gave two cents.'

'But you never married Mr Goldman.'

'So?' Beryl bridled. 'Big deal. What's marriage? Maggie says in the Bible it never said marriage was a legal thing, anyways. Listen. His family was strict Orthodox. He couldn't get married to a woman who wasn't Jewish, see?' Sometimes he gave Beryl a little extra money when he'd had a good week and she'd fold it up and tuck it carefully into a corner of her pocket. 'No matter what his family thinks, I've held on to him,' she exclaimed gleefully.

As Alice closed the door she could hear her mother's voice continuing. After a while Beryl would go to bed wearing a nylon nightgown over a black brassiere, and Mr Goldman would stroke her forehead to soothe her chronic headache before quietly leaving for his room at his brother-in-law's house. On weekends Mr Goldman slept at Beryl's, but he always ate at a café near the laundromat except on the High Holidays which he spent with relatives.

It didn't bother her that Mr Goldman's family would not receive her, Beryl said, or that she'd never been to his brother-in-law's house in Kerrisdale. Years before, when Mr Goldman's mother had died, Beryl had not gone to the funeral, but a couple of weeks afterwards Mr Goldman had carried home a large carton.

Beryl had reared up from the couch. 'What's that? The family jewels?'

Mr Goldman had wiped his forehead with a handkerchief. 'Some books for the kids.'

'Books?'

Alice had run and pulled open the box and even David had tottered over to touch the books with his fat baby hands. There was an old set of *The Book of Knowledge* encyclopedia with gold letters on the spines.

Beryl had lit a cigarette. 'Just don't clutter up the living room with those things,' she'd called out, coughing and motioning with one arm. 'Put them away somewhere.' Beryl hated books and even words themselves roused her ire. Whenever she wrote a letter she had to pore over Mr Goldman's newspaper to locate the words she wanted so she could spell them correctly.

'His family grabbed everything when Goldie's mother died,' Beryl explained to Alice. 'All he got was a box of old books. He's too soft, you know. People take advantage. His brother and sister cleaned up. They got everything.' She gulped at her tea. 'They made sure nothing would ever come to me or David.' Every once in a while she'd make a list of all the things Mr Goldman's mother must have owned. 'Who got the diamond engagement ring?' she'd call out. 'Who got her watch?'

CHAPTER TWO

THE BUS CREPT ALONG like a mechanical animal desperately traversing dangerous urban terrain, the flickering interior lights alternately shining on to the pale, tired faces of its passengers and thrusting them into darkness. Spiky drops of rain twisted down the windowpanes, like translucent wires cutting the wavering buildings outside into dark shapes, as Alice and Wendy sat together near the back door of the rattling vehicle on Friday night.

'Do you want to come shopping with me?' Wendy asked. Her eyelashes bent neatly upwards because, after she brushed on mascara, she crimped her sticky lashes with a curved metal instrument.

Later, in Eskin's dress shop, Alice observed Wendy peering at her own image in a mirror, drawing her thin, beige eyebrows together in concentration. 'It needs a necklace or something,' she pronounced in her quick voice. Alice admired Wendy's colouring; her light brown hair, so tidy and glossy, and her rosy skin. She herself sometimes wished to be that kind of girl, wonderfully normal in appearance, pleasantly and moderately complexioned in contrast to her own excessively ethnic darkness. Alice figured she was almost as hirsute as a Mediterranean woman. It wasn't fair. Just WHO had her father been? Why hadn't her mother taken these terrible consequences into account before she'd recklessly conceived? The saleswoman reappeared with a string of opalescent pink beads which she fastened around Wendy's neck.

'I don't know.' Wendy stared with dissatisfaction at the black pullover and skirt she was trying on. 'What do you think, Alice?'

Beryl chose Alice's clothes from the Salvation Army store on Lonsdale, explaining it was a waste of money to buy new garments when the rich cast away perfectly good clothing before it was even worn out. Right now Alice wore one of Beryl's finds: a wool skirt nubbed with tiny lumps, a feature which meant it had cost plenty at one time according to Beryl. Alice had been out of work for six months after quitting high school and she still owed her mother money for the cost of her lodgings. So Beryl took her daughter's paycheque, doling out enough for cigarettes, bus fare and adding a few extra dollars she called mad money. During these transactions, Beryl's face was desperately concentrated on her task. 'I'm teaching you how to manage money,' she'd announce importantly, laying bills and coins in Alice's palm while they sat at the kitchen table.

'Try the red sweater,' Alice said while she mulled over the question of whether or not physiognomy dictated destiny. It seemed important and yet Lawrence said Paul Morel sought more than mere appearance, an innate quality of being that a woman could not train into her soul.

Wendy disappeared behind the curtain of the fitting booth and Alice listened to the slide of wool on nylon, the rattle of the hanger on the hook and the hiss of the zipper. It was only the man who knew what this remarkable, truly womanly quality was and whether it was present at all. Paul's girlfriend Miriam had been weighed in the balance and found wanting; she was too spiritual, preoccupied with soulish things and given to private ecstasies. Alice looked idly at the floor littered with bits of lint and thread. She couldn't help liking Miriam, but what if this meant she herself suffered from the same faults and therefore her own judgement was suspect and corrupt? She might even be one of those women Paul's mother despised, one who wanted to suck the very soul from a man.

'It's sort of a cherry-red, don't you think?' Wendy called out as she emerged from the fitting room and turned slowly in tiny steps.

Alice knew women were always in danger of being looked at from behind: there was the possibility that a zipper might gape or cloth might be caught in a cleft of flesh. Alice had actually seen this occur to a woman as she chattered innocently to friends, unaware of the humiliating state of her clothing. Women had to be on guard against this kind of thing; a strap could tumble out of a sleeveless dress or a stain might appear on the back of a skirt.

Wendy was flushed and triumphant. 'I'll take it!' she cried before whirling into the changing booth. 'You should try on something too,' she called out, passing the sweater through the curtain to the saleswoman.

Alice wandered obediently over to the clothes rack, hoping she might find something that would change her into someone more like Wendy.

'You need to brighten yourself up,' Wendy encouraged.

She told Alice she should open a charge account at Eskin's and pay a little on her account every week. As they walked along the side of the road Wendy swung her box back and forth and automobiles rushing around the corner swept them with headlights.

'You should get out. Do things,' Wendy advised. 'My fiancé saw you at Woolworth's. He said you were a nice-looking girl but you didn't make the best of yourself.'

Wendy taught her to rub colour into her cheeks so her cheekbones looked higher. Fired with an artist's fervour, Wendy stared at Alice as if she were a blank canvas, making Alice sit on a straight-backed chair in her bedroom while she walked around her consideringly. 'Okay. You need Opal foundation and Opal tan for your nose. No offence, but that'll make it look smaller.'

'Really?'

'Sure!' Wendy lit a cigarette and leaned against her chest of drawers. 'Before I started my chin exercises, I had a round chin. Not really a double chin, but it COULD have become one.' She balanced her cigarette in an ashtray on the dresser. 'Now I do my exercises every day,' she said, placing one hand on top of her skull and straining her head forward in a snake-like movement.

Alice watched wonderingly. The body was important, it was

more than a receptacle containing the mind and spirit. That latter sort of view was limited and prudish and she scorned it right along with Lawrence.

Alice met Wendy's fiancé who was a short, thin man with a narrow face and a mocking smile. On Friday nights Don would pick Wendy up in front of the store and sometimes they took Alice along as well. When he drove Don slapped the steering wheel with the side of his hand in time to the music on the car radio, and Wendy tucked her head against his shoulder as he swerved in and out of traffic. Sometimes he worked nights at the hospital, where he was an orderly, and then Alice would stay at Wendy's where they'd lie in the dark, smoking cigarettes, just talking. Alice liked to hear her friend's passionate opinions about everything. Wendy even knew exactly what she wanted to have in her future kitchen. Alice was filled with amazement since the colour scheme of her own future was unknown to her.

'Don's sisters are helping me put together a recipe book of everything he likes to eat,' Wendy said.

Alice was interested in theories about men and their strange needs. Paul Morel's father had eaten his own child's treat from the pantry. What if she couldn't supply these necessary delicacies men seemed to crave? Her mother had once told her to put egg and breadcrumbs on fish and fry it for David and she'd mixed it together and desperately tried to stick slimy lumps on to the slippery white fish.

Now that Alice had undergone Wendy's self-improvement course, she wore only garments Wendy had approved. Her friend insisted Alice buy her clothes a size smaller than she'd worn before.

'Isn't it too tight?'

'It's your size, that's all. You always wore things too big.'

When she walked along the street with Wendy, men in cars cried out in appreciation.

'Men don't respect a woman who lays it all out on display,' Beryl said. 'You and that cow Wendy are just asking for it.

Don't ask me to identify your body when they find you in a ditch.'

Alice laughed scornfully, imagining a Victorian etching with the girl's white body by the side of the road and the mother turning away, back of hand to brow.

Her hair now back-combed and twirled into a sausage pinned up at the back, Alice lined her eyes with Egyptian Night and stroked Pink Peach on to her lips.

'You're headed right down,' Beryl warned.

David lay on his stomach on the living-room floor finishing the puzzle he was working on. He looked up wonderingly at the sound of the women's voices.

'Don't think you're going out tonight, that's for sure,' Beryl said.

'Why not?' Alice's head went up. She'd changed from her work clothes into a pale pink sweater and matching slacks.

'Because I say so, that's why. I'm still your mother.'

'That doesn't make any sense. I'm going out.'

'Out, out, out every night,' Beryl cried. 'With that Wendy dame.'

Alice's voice rose. 'I'm not. She's with her fiancé most of the time.'

Beryl slammed her cup on the table and weak tea splashed into the ashtray. 'Look what you made me do! How many fiancés has she had, that's what I want to know. She's got a reputation. I asked Maggie.'

'What are you talking about?' Alice moaned, pacing back and forth. 'What does Maggie know? She just sits in that store every day.'

Beryl breathed heavily. 'Don't you say anything about Maggie. SHE'S not the one running around the streets.'

On the television a cowboy crouched behind an overturned waggon and shot at tiny figures. Alice threw herself into the chair. 'What do you want? You don't like it when I sit at home and read and you don't like it when I go out. What do you want? Just tell me.'

Beryl's lips were tight. 'Don't you pull that act on me. A daughter's supposed to be a friend to her mother. You never tell me nothing. Why did I even have you?' The older woman gestured and ash from her cigarette scattered on to the carpet.

'Mom,' David begged in a wheedling voice, stamping out the sparks.

'You shut up.'

'What do you want me to tell you?' Alice closed her eyes and allowed her arms to hang limply over the sides of the chair.

'Forget it.'

'No,' Alice shook her head.

'A normal girl talks to her mother. She WANTS to spend time with her mother. She thinks about her family, not only about herself,' Beryl snarled.

A key turned in the lock. They were silent as Mr Goldman hung his hat on the hook and took his chair.

'How was your day, Goldie?' Beryl shot a glance at Alice.

'What an afternoon. Two of the machines broke down with laundry in them and I had to wring all the clothes out by hand.'

'Would you like a cup of tea? Alice'll make you one.' Beryl waved Alice to the kitchen.

Mr Goldman nodded and pinched the bridge of his nose. 'The repairmen finally came about six and they didn't have the right parts so they have to come back in the morning.'

'Don't pay the buggers.'

In the kitchen Alice pressed the kettle down on the burner so the water would boil faster. She could hear her mother telling Mr Goldman what he should have said to the repairmen. Wendy had Don's car tonight and she and Alice were going to a Chinese café where they'd eat egg rolls with plum sauce.

As she handed Mr Goldman a cup of tea with a slice of lemon, Alice found herself puzzling over Lawrence's phrase, 'dark loins of passion'. What exactly were loins? In what part of the body were they, or it, located? It seemed crucial to know.

'I'll be back early,' she called out, slinging her purse over her shoulder.

'You stay in!' Beryl yelled. Her face was scarlet, tears rose in her eyes and cords on her neck stood out. She jumped up and screamed, 'You give me worry, that's all you're good for; you and your fast friend. I told my doctor about you and you know what he said? And he's an educated man. He said there's one in every family.' Her eyes flashed and she stood with knees bent like a fighter in the ring.

'I'm only going out for a couple of hours,' Alice pleaded, trying to catch Mr Goldman's eye.

'Do you hear her talking back?' Beryl turned to Mr Goldman. 'Do you?' David put his hands over his ears. 'Do you see what kind of a daughter I have? Do YOU think she should go out?'

'Listen to your mother, Alice,' Mr Goldman looked up as Alice leaned against the door, swinging her purse.

'I don't believe this. All this fuss about nothing.' The light shone on the little droplets of hairspray in Alice's hair and her voice was choked and painful. 'This isn't a normal family.'

'Okay, that does it. Get to your room.' Beryl grabbed a cushion from the couch and kneaded it between her hands. 'I've had enough.' She threw the cushion across the room and it hit the base of a lamp so a puff of dust rose from the shade.

'I'm going out,' Alice repeated in a cold, controlled voice and placed her hand on the doorknob.

'Stop her, Goldie. Get her!' Beryl rushed towards the door and pressed her body against it, staring wildly at Alice. 'You're not leaving.'

'There's a back door, you know.'

'I'll lie in front of it,' Beryl gasped. 'Goldie can guard this one.'

Mr Goldman rose from his chair and walked quickly to the door. 'You do what your mother says. Your mother's nerves are bad enough!' He raised one hand warningly.

Alice stared back at him as he stood beside her mother, with his palm raised and his sensitive fingers bent slightly backwards. Her throat ached.

'Don't let her get past us, Goldie!'

Mr Goldman had always sat so quietly and reasonably in his chair, the descendant of rabbis.

Alice whirled and ran down the hall to her room. 'I'm young, you know,' she yelled, sobbing.

CHAPTER THREE

SOME NIGHTS the lure of the television overcame David, and he followed its seductive voice from his bedroom into the cold hallway, where he sneaked to the door of the living room and stared around the corner. From that angle he could see flat images dancing under the domed glass of the television screen, surrounded with magical, bluish light in the darkened room.

He was a mesmerized child, attached to television which had been his companion since birth when Mr Goldman had bought the heavy console for Beryl who'd complained of loneliness. David had learned to sit quietly on the floor, just a few feet from the set, as the television marked out the hours of the day with *Rin Tin Tin*, *The Three Stooges*, *The Twilight Zone* and cartoons. The programmes changed with the seasons and punc-tuated David's life with their regular rhythmic revolutions.

Alice always went to bed when the late movie came on because her mother had told her that that was her own time alone with Mr Goldman. However, Alice had to marshal all her will to snap her book shut and turn off the light when she lay in her bedroom. Otherwise she might read until morning before dragging her body out of bed when the alarm went off, forcing it to get on the bus to fill the Woolworth's counter with stock, then smile at customers.

She lay in the dark listening to the rain. When she rolled up her blind in the morning, she knew she'd see the wet back porch with a bag of garbage on it surrounded by the cans, rinds and torn paper Beryl would order her to pick up after work. A bleak greyish downpour would soak everything – the tall grass in the back yard was bent under the weight of the water, the seed heads beaded with droplets and the grass spears gleaming with wetness. Alice heard David's door open slowly, then the sound of his footsteps, and pictured him sneaking down the hallway, creeping towards the television like a somnambulist moving unconsciously towards his desire, mouth open.

'Are you out of bed, David?' Alice heard her mother's voice, thick with cigarettes.

The footsteps stopped.

'Answer. Is that you?' The sofa creaked and Alice heard the sound of her mother's cup being set down.

There was a thud of small bare feet in the hallway; David's door shut with a click and the springs of his bed squeaked.

'I'm not going to stand for this any longer.' Beryl's thongs slapped down the hall and David's door was flung open so the handle hit the wall with a bang.

'Don't hit me! Don't hit me!'

'Don't!' Slap. 'Get!' Slap. 'Out!' Slap. 'Of!' Slap. 'Bed!' Slap. David howled. His door was slammed and the thongs flip-flopped back into the living room.

'Was that really necessary?' Mr Goldman asked.

Alice crept softly across the hall into David's bedroom and comforted him while his cries turned to gasps.

'Are you kidding? The kid's been getting up night after night,' Beryl replied. A match scratched along the rough strip on the side of the blue and white striped matchbox. 'What do you expect me to do about it? YOU just sit there and do nothing.' The television dial clicked angrily around the channels. 'If I just sat on my ass like you the kid would go wild.'

Back in her own room, Alice knelt by the door and leaned her head against the moulding. She couldn't hear David any more so she assumed he was listening as well. Sometimes when Alice gazed at her brother she felt helpless. His small body appeared tensely defensive and his hands trembled. At the beach in the summer he'd crouch shivering at the edge of the water, afraid of the waves. Surely that wasn't normal in a child? When he had to read aloud he stammered and made mistakes. Alice would sit at the kitchen table to help him with his schoolwork, but when she saw his small hands grasping the book and heard him guessing desperately in his high, child's voice, she'd want to hide her face and weep. 'Good,' she'd encourage as David traced his grubby finger along a line of words, but it pained her to see her brother so wretched and fearful, so daunted by the school primer.

'I don't want my son hit.'

Mr Goldman usually avoided arguments, preferring to read his newspaper, holding the pages up like a shield while he waited until Beryl's rage had subsided.

'Sure. Why don't YOU stay here all day with him?' Beryl shrieked.

'I support him.'

'Oh, God, now hold that over me. You pay the rent so you can tell me what to do, is that it? Maggie told me that's why men think they can do whatever they want.'

'You're glad to get the money.'

'So? Don't I need it? Didn't I have your precious son?'

Silence.

'I know what you and your family call me. Maggie told me. Filth. You call me filth.' Beryl paused, gasping, trying to catch her breath.

'You don't know what you're talking about.'

Something broke. Was it one of the pearly orange mugs her mother always used? Alice wondered, crouched in the dark.

'Don't give me that crap. You think you can walk in here like King Tut and tell me what to do. Sure, you're a big wheel, just because you can sit there wasting your time with those crossword puzzles all day and all night. You think that gives you the right to lord it over me.'

Mr Goldman groaned.

'I can't take it,' Beryl screamed. 'All the pressure and stress. I don't get no appreciation.'

Alice watched the light under the door.

'If you don't like the way I bring up David, why don't you just get out?' Beryl sobbed.

'That's not a bad idea,' Mr Goldman said coldly.

Holding her breath Alice heard his footsteps cross to the door and her mother's sobs grew louder – then the front door closed. She leapt back into bed just before her bedroom door flew open.

'I suppose you were having a good listen.'

Alice blinked.

Beryl flopped down beside the bed. 'Goldie's gone,' she said. 'Maybe he'll come back.'

'Fat lot you know. He's stubborn. Quiet but stubborn.' Beryl gazed at the ash on her cigarette. 'Do you have an ashtray?'

Alice shook her head.

'Never mind. I'll just put it on my shoe.' Beryl tapped her cigarette and a little pile of ash fell on to the sole of the thong she held up like a tray. 'You have to give me your whole cheque now. We need it for the rent, no more of that mad money business. Just never start with men,' Beryl added, glaring fiercely. 'I always had a good figure, that was my problem. I never met a man who didn't make a pass at me.'

Mr Goldman could come back some night, Alice thought; there could be a knock at the door and he'd walk back in and hang up his hat and no one would say anything. Her mother's nature would be sweeter, chastened by their separation. Beryl might convert and she and Mr Goldman could be married under an embroidered canopy. The house would be full of new relatives, dancing.

What a waste of time her life with Goldie had been, Beryl decided. She had been lively and amusing, she told Alice the next evening. 'People think I'm comical,' she snarled. 'I can dance. I like to go out. What does Goldie like to do? Nothing. Maggie says if it hadn't been for him who knows where I might be today,' Beryl commented as she looked through her box of photographs. 'Lookit.' She held a picture in which she sat on an upholstered bench in front of pale drapes. Her thin young face was surrounded by curled brown hair and her laughing mouth was dark and large with lipstick above a tight white sweater and a skirt pulled up above crossed knees. 'If I knew then what I know now,' she murmured, gazing admiringly at her former self. 'Jeez!'

Beryl and Maggie had decided the break with Mr Goldman was a fresh start, another chance at the glories Beryl deserved because of the perfection of her body and the longing of her spirit. 'I had gold between my legs and didn't know it,' Beryl screeched, laughing boisterously at her children's shocked faces.

CHAPTER FOUR

'YOU'RE STILL YOUNG,' Maggie informed Beryl. 'Why waste your time? Get out. Meet people.'

When Alice returned from work she found Beryl hunched at the vanity table in her bedroom, wearing her blue chenille robe stained with face powder. Eyes screwed up in concentration, she daubed into little pots and smeared liquids on her face. The silver backing of the mirror was worn away so her reflection was fractured in places by absences and spidery lines.

'You're babysitting tonight. I'm going out,' she cried.

'What about me?' Alice asked, dropping her books on the floor and settling herself beside them.

Beryl held her mouth stiffly open and rubbed scarlet lipstick around the edge before pressing her lips on a tissue. 'You're always out. I'm going to the Legion.' Beryl spat into a block of mascara and stirred the black paste with a tiny brush.

'When are you coming back?' Alice persisted.

'When I feel like it. I need to have some life,' Beryl lashed out, pulling a black nylon blouse from the mound of garments on her bed. Then she snatched up a hairbrush and dragged it across her head but the bristles caught in the matted strands.

'Don't you think Mr Goldman will come back?'

'Who cares? David's all he thinks about,' Beryl cried. 'Anyways, what business is it of yours?' she demanded menacingly. 'Maggie put her finger on it. He's not my type.' Opening her jewel box she held up rhinestone earrings. 'These'll go good.'

When she emerged from her bedroom Alice and David were clicking plastic discs along the Snakes and Ladders board. The brisk tap of high heels drew their eyes to the hallway where Beryl stood erect and triumphant with her blouse puffed out from a tight black skirt that rode above bare, unshaven legs and her feet pinched into black, toeless shoes with patent bows on the sides. She wore a flared, blue jacket while a spray of rhinestones blazed from each ear. 'Not bad, eh?' she called as she spun out the door.

Later Alice drew the covers up to David's neck and he turned over on his side obediently. David's gaze was watchful and intelligent but he was so young. Alice smoothed his hair which was rough and dry against her palm. She felt she should utter some kind of warning but didn't know what to say, so she kept silent. In the empty living room a clock ticked loudly; she propped her book on her knees and read until she heard a car door slam and the sound of voices.

'I've brought the navy!' Beryl called out, flinging the door open. A tall, thin man was with her, waving a bottle, and a second fellow with a thick body like a boxer tripped over the doorjamb. 'This is Liam,' Beryl gestured towards the first man, 'and his pal Donal. Irish Navy. Just off the boat, eh, fellas?'

'My daughter,' Beryl swept her arm towards Alice and one ankle bent so she staggered a little. 'Holy cow!' Beryl exclaimed. 'I'm not used to these high heels.' The tall man took her arm to steady her. Donal sat heavily beside Alice. 'Your mother's a lovely dancer,' he said. Then the cork flew out of the bottle of Dubonnet and the men poured it into tumblers.

'Hey! That's not apple juice, you know,' Beryl yelled gaily, stretching her red mouth as she laughed.

Alice tasted hers and made a face.

'Does your daughter not drink?'

Beryl flopped in the chair and the ashtray on the little table slid and hit an empty mug. 'Don't worry about her,' she said airily.

Liam lolled on the arm of the big chair above Beryl. 'You with a grown daughter. It's amazing.'

'That's enough blarney! I'm Irish too, you know,' Beryl cried, kicking her foot in his direction.

'You've got Irish eyes,' Liam agreed, smirking as he draped his long arm over the back of the chair.

'*When Irish eyes are smiling,*' Donal sang. 'You look like one of the Black Irish,' he murmured to Alice, putting his pale, freckled face close to hers.

Alice held her drink in her lap, swilling the sweet liquid around and staring at it.

'*Stood a young lad, Kevin Barry, just because he would not lie . . .* ' Beryl and Liam's voices grew in volume. '*Mother, mother!*' they sang, their eyes wet.

Donal sighed. 'You've got beautiful hips for childbearing,' he said, tumbling over.

Beryl and Liam shrieked with laughter. Then Beryl shot out of her chair, snapped her fingers and wriggled her hips, her blouse pulled up at the back. 'Let's get this party going,' she yelled, her face flushed.

'You've half-killed us already!' Liam groaned. 'We're no match for you.'

Beryl crouched in front of the record-player. 'I was the best jitterbugger at the Y dances. I won all the prizes,' she shouted, yanking a record from a sleeve and setting it on the turntable.

Donal lurched up and jiggled his knees, wagging Alice's hand. Alice watched Beryl and Liam whirling professionally. He slid her mother between his legs and back upright and she twirled expertly under his arm. The record stopped and Donal's eyelids flew up. There was sweat on his upper lip as he stepped carefully forward, reaching out like a blind man for the couch. 'Give me a little more in my glass, won't you?'

Liam threw himself down and hauled Beryl into his lap. 'Now don't you get fresh!' Beryl struggled when Liam's arms looped around her. 'Bloody great Irishman,' she laughed, her eyes wild. 'What's a girl to do?'

'Just enjoy it. Drink's a curse but life's worse!'

Beryl and Liam doubled up laughing while Donal lifted a glass to his full lips and poured the drink down his chin.

Alice walked to the kitchen and snatched up a tea towel that lay in a heap. She handed it to Donal without a word. In Lawrence's novel Alice would be a woman quivering with life and meaning. She wouldn't be blanked out by the vigour of others. Each moment would rush towards some kind of splendid culmination.

'Oh, he's taken with your daughter. I can tell you that.' Liam gazed at his friend who sat on the couch like a statue.

'We're hot stuff in this family,' Beryl cried.

In a novel, Alice thought frantically, she might dash out into a garden and Donal, who would not be drunk, would find her and utter marvellous, piercing, enigmatic statements. Liam poured a stream of Dubonnet into Beryl's glass. 'Drink up,' he encouraged.

'How long is your ship in?' Alice asked suddenly.

'Five days,' Donal said, sitting up and placing his hands on his thighs. *'Then home again, home again, jiggety-jog.'*

Beryl shrieked when Liam clasped her in his arms. 'You'll not let me go home lonely, will you?' he crooned.

'Jiggety-jog,' Donal repeated sadly. 'There's no rhyme to it.' His face was very white.

'God!' Liam cried, springing forward and pulling Donal up. 'Excuse us, girls.' Liam slung his friend's arm over his shoulder. 'Where's the toilet?'

'Never mind him,' Liam told Beryl when they came back after banging around the bathroom. 'He'll do fine. Where were we?'

'I heard a noise,' David said, standing in the hall.

'It's just a sick man. Go back to bed,' Beryl said sharply.

'Is my dad sick?'

'No. Just go to bed.'

The child turned.

Donal lurched up and pawed at the air. 'I could break everything in this room. I could break this chair right over your head,' he cried, staring.

'It's all right, lad.' Liam spoke soothingly, rising from his chair but Donal panted and waved his arms, knocking the rabbit ears off the television.

'He's off,' Liam pronounced.

Alice grabbed the rabbit ears.

'There's no stopping him now,' Liam cried, guiding his friend to the door. 'It's been a lovely evening, though.' He stopped and ran back to pick up the bottle of Dubonnet. 'No point wasting it, is there?' The door closed on Donal's wounded voice.

Beryl crouched in her chair. 'What're you looking at?' She regarded Alice accusingly. 'You don't know nothing about men. I can give you some pointers.' Beryl sipped at her glass. 'Like tonight. You just sat there like a block of wood and I had to keep everything going.'

Alice swung her foot back and forth and looked at the stains and bits of fluff on the rug. Beryl usually saved the vacuuming for Alice's weekend chore. The machine lay tangled in a closet and had to be dragged out like a stubborn animal. Alice stared with determination at the discoloured rug while Beryl's voice continued.

'I mean it. You're cold, that's your problem. You get that from your creep of a father.'

'I'm going to bed.'

'I was too kind. Too soft. The opposite of you. I remember a friend of mine forced me to have sex while his mother was upstairs asleep.' Beryl paused significantly. 'I couldn't yell because I didn't want her to be upset. After all, he was her son.'

Alice held on to the doorjamb and looked at her mother who was transfixed by memories of sacrifice.

'He had a cast on his leg at the time,' Beryl mused, lifting her glass to smeared, scarlet lips.

CHAPTER FIVE

DINNER WAS WAITING for Alice under an overturned plate in the oven, and she jabbed at the heap of macaroni surrounded by pale, congealed sauce while listening to her mother talk to Maggie on the telephone.

'Why quarrel?' Beryl burst out. 'What's the point? Live and let live, that's what I say.'

On the living-room floor, David extracted coils and bits of wire from an old radio. He haunted the alleys, poking into garbage cans and peering into big industrial containers.

'I'm just too forgiving,' Beryl sighed, blowing out a match and puffing on a fresh cigarette.

Alice ran hot water into the sink to wash the dishes, spearing the bar of soap and holding it under the hot, gushing tap to form oily, quivering bubbles. She glanced out the back window where a string around some sticks marked off the plot Beryl planned to use as a vegetable garden. Everyone in the family was supposed to dig a row a day, she'd said, and David had gouged a deep hole in the centre, abandoning the shovel which lay rusting in the grass.

'I want this place spic-and-span when I get back from where I'm going,' Beryl yelled. 'And don't say nothing about last night, either,' she commanded, 'if you know what's good for you.' She stamped out, slamming the door.

Alice smoothed out the bedspread on the couch and wiped the ashes from the table; the bedspread's colour sickened her and the rows of clumped chenille rasped at the tips of her fingers. Her dustcloth wiped a damp swath on gritty surfaces which immediately returned to their former scratched dimness.

'Who's coming?' David asked. 'The sick man?'

Later Beryl marched in followed by Mr Goldman and Alice stood watching as he embraced David. Beryl tossed her coat over the back of her chair, flopping down as if exhausted. 'What's on TV?' she demanded.

Mr Goldman nodded to Alice.

'The child needs a father,' Beryl murmured, switching on the set.

'Why hold grudges?' she cried to Maggie the next day, but she was subdued for a time and started a new project with her photographs, pulling them out of her blue metal trunk and trying to put them in order.

Alice explained her secret kinship with Mr Goldman to Wendy. 'Of course he keeps his deepest feelings hidden,' she told her friend. Mr Goldman had a horror of vulgarity and falseness, Alice said, intent on making Wendy understand Mr Goldman was her true parent while her mother could claim only biological connection. Alice went on to say Mr Goldman's reserve hid the purity and beauty of his soul from the stunning power of Beryl's wrath. He protected Alice by not revealing his secret affection for her since Beryl, like a bitter queen, demanded total allegiance.

At Wendy's house, someone was always heating something on the stove or checking a dish in the oven. 'Have you tried it wrapped in bacon? With melted cheese?' they'd call. Alice had never known anyone who enjoyed food. Wendy and Mrs Gregg taught Alice to make pancakes but the results of her efforts were flaccid and deformed. She walked calmly to their bathroom and wept into a towel. Everyone in the Gregg family could cook, even the men. Sundays, the kitchen was fragrant with the mingled perfumes of roast beef and apple pies and Mrs Gregg and Wendy set out buttered potatoes, bright peas and multicoloured salad. A pitcher of dark gravy stood beside the platter of meat and there were sliced dills and tiny onions as well. Alice lifted her fork to her mouth wonderingly; she'd always thought of eating as an accident of evolution, an awkward and mechanical animal act. She'd hoped someday there would be a pill invented (didn't the magazines prophesy such a thing was possible?) that would do away with the base need altogether. Yet the Greggs seized serving dishes and spooned out second helpings.

Mrs Gregg had been born on a farm in Hungary, arriving in Canada as a bewildered girl and afterwards marrying Al Gregg, a truck driver she met at a church social. When their children were young his right eye had been blown out by an exploding, hot water heater which had puckered the side of his face and seared one shoulder.

'He was never the same,' Wendy said.

'His face, you mean?'

'His brain.'

'He used to be different?'

'He used to be normal,' Wendy stated crisply, while she pulled on her stockings. 'He never takes a bath. I don't know how Mum stands it. I'd divorce him!' Wendy cried.

Mrs Gregg cooked for a restaurant but Mr Gregg hadn't worked since his accident. Wendy's brother, Billy, helped the family by living in the basement and paying room and board. It was clear to Alice that Mrs Gregg was a saint. She came home from work late and put her feet up on a hassock, exposing legs that were hairless and shiny. When she had a bath she washed the bathroom walls. To discourage her, Alice and Wendy purchased a large bottle of bubble bath for her birthday, but Mrs Gregg just rinsed her Sunday stockings in the perfumed suds.

'She's so dumpy. I'll never get like her,' Wendy would vow, standing at the mirror and sucking in her stomach.

'She's motherly-looking,' Alice said.

'Fat, you mean. I'd die if I looked like that.'

'She doesn't care about those things.' Mrs Gregg attended a church that forbade worldliness in dress and attitude.

'Nobody wants boobs hanging down to their waist. She stays fat because she hates sex.'

Alice realized this was a serious thing, like hating life or being out of step with the universe. D. H. Lawrence said once a woman had flamed with sexual joy it was as if she were a lamp which, once lit, would burn forever. A woman had to wait for this dazzling illumination.

'She once made Dad pay her five dollars for it.'

'Are you kidding?'

'No. It's true. She got so fed up with him always bugging her about it that she made him pay.' Wendy's voice was excited and high-pitched.

Alice stared at Wendy, unable to imagine what Lawrence would have said about Mrs Gregg's behaviour.

'And even then she just let him have a feel. No kidding. It's a wonder us kids are normal. Mum just thinks people should be religious and forget about anything else.'

Alice thought it was a shame Mrs Gregg didn't know sex was religious. She didn't need to give up one for the other since everything should fuse together – sex, religion and nature.

Billy Gregg received frequent calls. Occasionally he announced the names of women whose messages were welcome but others had to rely on luck to catch him at home between shifts. Mrs Gregg insisted she'd seen one young woman waiting beneath the lamppost at the end of the street, hoping he'd appear. He and his friends sauntered into the back yard to lift weights, stripping off shirts and revealing great chests and backs while they talked about bulk and definition. Wendy said he'd been a thin boy but now he stood in the hallway, gazing into the mirror, twitching his pectorals. 'I'm going to need a brassiere soon, Maw,' he'd call out gaily.

Wendy and Alice talked quietly in the darkness of Wendy's room at night while from the adjacent living room they could hear the murmur of Mrs Gregg's voice imploring God to save her children's souls. Every evening after the others had gone to bed she knelt in the living room, her face shining with cold cream. Mrs Gregg had a sweet, pointed face and a long, thin nose with delicate, reddened nostrils. Her cheeks were fuzzed with fine, almost invisible hair.

'How?' Alice asked when Wendy confided she'd had what the sex manuals called a climax. Alice had puzzled over this glorious mystery described in Lawrence's books.

'Don was just fooling around,' Wendy said lazily as she inhaled and exhaled smoke in a sigh.

'Tell!' Alice shrieked, but Wendy laughed and would say nothing more.

In the morning Alice and Wendy performed exercises they'd learned from a pocket book that said chests and hips must be identical in circumference, with waists ten inches less. Working towards that perfect ideal they stretched and bumped across the floor. Wendy's brother and his friends called plain women 'dogs' and Alice knew exactly what kind of animals they meant. She hoped they'd never guess it was only her own cleverness and vigilance that prevented them from calling her a dog too; she never passed a mirror without checking to see if some abomination was present – a stalk of hair sticking up, for example, or food gummed between teeth.

As she and Wendy rolled their hips from side to side the back door burst open and Billy slammed his empty lunchpail on the counter crying he needed food. He was a deckhand on a tugboat and after work the pungent reek of diesel oil emanated from his stained clothes and skin. 'Maw!' he called again.

'Yes, yes. Just wait. Your sister will give you some pancakes,' Mrs Gregg said, her voice suggesting an infinity of female patience while she poured Billy a cup of tea from the brown pot that stood on the warming shelf above the stove.

'Here. Shut up,' Wendy said, banging a plate in front of her brother. 'Why can't you get your own?'

'She's mean to me, Maw,' Billy grimaced comically, cutting his food into large pieces dripping with syrup, holding the fork in dark, greasy fingers. He drank several cups of strong tea before going downstairs to his basement suite to have a shower.

Mrs Gregg sighed and smiled. 'He's such a bear.'

'A pig, you mean,' Wendy snapped, wiping the table with rapid motions and rinsing out the cloth under the tap. They could hear the sound of Billy's stereo thumping beneath the floor.

This was real family life, Alice thought. Loving insults, delicious food, and a mother who laughed forgivingly at her children's bad behaviour. After breakfast, Wendy took a long bath with milk powder in the water to feed her skin and Mrs Gregg lay down for a nap, resting in preparation for the night's work. Alice sat on the couch and waited, leaning her head against the crocheted doily in variegated green cotton, fashioned by Mrs Gregg's friend and neighbour, Mrs Kerkold. The flowered curtains had been pulled back from the picture window and the floors were clean and polished. When Billy wandered into the living room Alice tried not to look at his bare chest with its curled, glinting hair. He was always rubbing his chest and gazing at his body from different angles and his attitude seemed to transfer itself to her so she too was drawn to contemplate his form with its delicate planes and fine skin.

'Do you want to listen to a new record I got?' Billy asked and Alice nodded, inarticulate with shyness. Wishing she possessed the careless élan of the truly popular, she followed him down the back stairs.

Knotty pine panelling covered the walls of his suite and through an open door she could see a corner of an unmade bed and a portion of orange shag rug. Mrs Gregg and Wendy were convinced Billy spirited women into the basement at night and sneaked them out in the morning. He flopped one arm on to the back of the couch behind Alice and closed his eyes after setting a record on his powerful hifi. Alice was aware of the music's rhythmic throb passing into the house above, moving in waves beneath Wendy's bath and Mrs Gregg's bed. Then she heard pounding on the back door and Billy strode through the blackness of the unfinished part of the basement.

'What's going on?' Wendy cried. 'Why is the door locked?' Billy began to reply in a placating tone. 'Someone phoned you, but she might have hung up by now,' Wendy interrupted.

'Was there really anyone on the phone?' Alice whispered when she and Wendy were upstairs.

'Are you kidding?'

Alice and Wendy liked to sit in the kitchen listening to Mrs Gregg and Mrs Kerkold. Mrs Kerkold lived across the lane and had been a widow for years. Men were always pressing their heavy bodies on to women, the two older women said while they ate mounds of fried onions. Mrs Kerkold, a heavy woman, slapped her hand on the table. 'When I was young, I couldn't look at a man without getting pregnant,' she boasted. She and Mrs Gregg told of a friend's husband who went to sleep directly after sex was finished, lying between his wife's legs despite her bad veins. They spoke of men the way early missionaries referred to their charges, with tenderness and contempt, marvelling at their strange, childish thoughts and actions. Alice and Wendy glanced at each other and smiled. A laughing girl could find herself crushed and varicosed under the weight of a man, but they knew this was not going to happen to them.

CHAPTER SIX

MILKSHAKE MIXERS buzzed and cash drawers shot out stuffed with bills at Woolworth's 'Two for One' sale, where shoppers dragged at the streams of plastic belts and heaps of viscose knit dresses packed into clear plastic cylinders displayed on Alice's counter. She could see Mr Fordham signalling to her.

'The gal who usually washes dishes is sick, Alice,' Mr Fordham said in his hard, rattling voice after she pushed her way towards him. 'Will you help us out?'

She didn't like Mr Fordham to say her name and wondered how Paul Morel could have enjoyed working for the firm that sold ugly elastic stockings, and then even managed to paint and study at night. Pondering her own lack of delight in the ordinary things Lawrence considered so important, she slid plates into the racks of the dishwasher, a stainless steel dome behind the lunch counter, its racks moving along rollers into the hot, steaming centre of the machine. At the other side she pulled up the curved metal door and yanked out the hot plates, cups and glasses. The staff loved and respected Paul and bought him presents honouring his nature as an artist. Steam softened the lines of Egyptian Night around her eyes as she stacked the burning dishes in round wells where a spring lifted them so the top plate was always ready for the waitresses to snatch up. Behind her, Mr Fordham, Chuck and Brenda sat on the red leatherette lunch-counter stools.

'Take a break, Alice,' she heard Chuck call out and when she turned her head Alice saw he was alone so she moved to the empty spot beside him, plucking a cigarette from the red packet he held out, pulling her head back from the sudden flame of his lighter. Chuck's wrists, emerging from his white shirt cuffs, were thin, his skin, greyish white. Smoke rushed down Alice's throat as she listened to Chuck outlining his plan to become assistant manager by the following year. When he'd first arrived at the store he was assigned in turn to several of the most experienced women who had trained him, while cataloguing his faults in the staffroom.

'What's your ambition?' he asked now.

Another of those questions that could never be answered, Alice thought, examining the smoke seeping from the cigarette's filter. People would reel back with consternation at a truthful confession.

'You should have some plan,' Chuck informed her, lowering his voice. 'Don't you want to be head girl when Carol retires?'

Could this go on forever? Alice wondered, picturing herself at age thirty or even forty bobbing from behind one of Woolworth's counters, still clad in her faded smock. Her face would be stiff with misery, her hair permed into dry, crisp waves.

Chuck leaned towards Alice, advising her to start thinking about her future. 'You've got potential,' he said. 'I've never heard you ask for a drag of a cigarette like the other girls. You say puff, not drag,' he continued, his voice encouraging.

Diane spun on to the seat next to Chuck. 'Whaddya whispering about?' She turned to Alice. 'Is he giving you all that crap about making a plan?' Diane was a new clerk, a favourite of Mr Fordham's.

Chuck flushed.

'Just enjoy life,' Diane cried, her skirt pulled up over white, pimpled thighs. She laughed while Chuck's prominent Adam's apple bounced up and down.

'What a day!' she waved at the waitress. 'Mr Fordham's going crazy. He's never seen toys sell this fast.'

Diane twitched her eyebrows and rolled her eyes as Chuck walked away. 'He's scared of women,' she confided. 'Hey, Irene, gimme one of those Long Johns.' The waitress set down a chocolate-covered oblong and Alice slipped around the counter to load more dishes into the machine. As her hands worked, she gazed into her future. What if she didn't die at a romantically young age? What if she continued to live on and on but everything else stayed the same?

When she reached home, she bent to collect the weathered fliers on the front porch, her eyes sweeping over the peeling entrance and the grit caught in the cracks. A smell of cigarette smoke and boiled potatoes gusted out when she crossed the threshold and saw Beryl, body alert and face avid, sitting in Mr Goldman's chair. Two young men wearing navy blue suits leaned forward nervously on the edge of the couch.

'Here's my daughter,' Beryl said, waving a thin arm with exaggerated graciousness. 'Let's see what she thinks.'

The two men were curiously alike.

'They're Mormons,' Beryl cried as she lit another cigarette and shook out the match. 'They gave me this book. Free.' She wagged the volume back and forth and passed it to Alice who listened as the men talked about the angel Moroni, supposing embarrassing beliefs were the true sign of religious conviction. In Mrs Gregg's church there was similar evidence of deep faith because its members wore ugly clothes and said things like, 'Praise the Lord,' out loud.

'What about sex? Can Mormons have sex?' Beryl swivelled her head to make sure Alice was taking this in.

'Not before marriage.'

Beryl sat straight up in triumph. 'Do you really think God is against people having a good fuck?' she demanded.

One of the men doubled up in a spasm of high-pitched laughter and the other flushed.

'I don't think He cares about all that stuff,' Beryl said coolly, blowing smoke out of her nostrils, pleased with the effect of her remark.

The men looked at her helplessly.

After they left, Alice glanced at the fliers in her hand. There was also a catalogue of night-school courses describing spring offerings and she flicked through its pages, noting that registration was just two days away. 'You think I should learn to type?' Alice asked her mother. Maybe Chuck was right and she'd end up like Irene or Doris.

'There's good money in typing,' Beryl mused as she stared

out the window. 'You should make the most of yourself.' The excitement of the men's visit had passed and she was falling into a depression, pulling her legs up into the chair and smoking listlessly. 'Tea,' she ordered in a flat voice, holding out her mug.

Alice went out to the kitchen and filled the kettle, jamming it into the sink by pushing aside the dirty dishes. She wasn't sure she had the manual dexterity needed by a typist. Cups often fell from her hands and shattered, or she twisted the knobs off radios while thinking about other things, oblivious to Beryl's conversation.

'Maggie says you should improve yourself,' her mother continued when Alice went back into the living room. 'Don't end up landed with some kid when you're young like I did. I had talent, you know,' she went on, her eyes brilliant with blame. 'You should have seen me play baseball. And they used to line up to dance with me. I don't know why you didn't get no talent that way. I had plenty but I didn't get no encouragement. You're lucky,' Beryl said. 'Take advantage of it,' she added, with a resentful glance at Alice. 'Are you listening?' The hair on Beryl's legs seemed electric with energy as she twisted her wide, knobbly feet.

When she warmed the teapot, Alice sluiced the hot water out the back door to avoid dumping it in the sink where spray would deflect from the dishes. A hamburger patty was drying out in the oven with a mound of mashed peas beside it. She would be practical, Alice vowed. She'd become a typist who would hurry down the street to deliver an important document, perhaps bumping into a writer with burning eyes.

CHAPTER SEVEN

AFTER SHE SPRINKLED WATER over her blue blouse, Alice touched the bottom of the iron with her fingertips. According to Wendy, clothes had to be freshly ironed each day and it simply wasn't good enough to do a week's ironing at once. Wendy herself pressed each garment just before she put it on, laying a damp tea towel over her slacks and slamming the hissing iron on to the cloth, while the smell of hot wool swarmed into the air.

'Don't just iron one thing, either,' Beryl yelled. 'That's waste. We're not made of money, are we, Goldie?'

Mr Goldman shrugged and chuckled politely before turning back to his paper and Alice tried to figure out if Mr Goldman actually thought Beryl's remarks were witty or if he was carefully humouring her, fearing some violent mood. He sat in his chair listening and doing crossword puzzles, his face gentle and composed in the light from the lamp that stood nearby. When the phone rang Alice flicked off the switch on the iron and dashed into the hall.

'There goes more electricity,' Beryl commented. Alice sat on the floor and lifted the receiver. It was Wendy, her voice thinner and weaker than usual as if she were calling from a great distance. 'What are you doing?' Alice asked Wendy. They always told each other everything, memorizing the contents of each other's closets, so they could make precise suggestions. 'Why don't you wear the off-white wool pants with that black blouse you wore when you went to the drive-in?' one would say to the other. Their lives seemed to flow together, without separation.

'Nothing,' Wendy said. 'Everybody's out.'

There was a pin jammed into a crack in the floorboards and Alice picked at it with her fingernail.

'I think I'm pregnant,' Wendy groaned.

Alice pressed her fingers against her ear and listened to her blood throbbing in tiny, rapid beats. 'Are you sure?' she asked, trying to keep her voice calm to avoid increasing her friend's alarm. Wendy said she was having a test but she was certain it would be positive. 'What does Don say?' Alice whispered. Wendy had obtained a rubber disc that was supposed to prevent conception and she'd carried it in a pale blue plastic case like a compact.

'He's scared.'

It was incomprehensible, Alice thought, that disaster could strike Wendy who was so undeserving of such punishment, so assured and practical. It was like some ridiculous equation. On one side was Wendy, full of energy and loveliness; on the other was immovable biological fact. This was like one of Mrs Gregg's stories Alice realized with a shock.

'Don't stay on that phone all night!' Beryl roared. 'I'm expecting an important call.'

Alice pushed the receiver against her ear. 'What will he do if you are?' Don, who was not pretty or graceful like Wendy, now held the only possibility of rescue.

'He says he doesn't know,' Wendy gasped.

'Sorry, the course is filled.'

Alice looked down at the woman who spoke.

The woman in the high-school auditorium repeated her statement. 'The typing course is filled, dear. You'll have to wait for next semester.'

Alice wandered away and examined notices on the bulletin board beside the varnished tables where teachers sat with record books. She was determined to take *something*. 'I'd like to sign up,' she declared to the teacher of a course called 'The Prophetic Novel'. He was a dark, bearded man in his late twenties who wore a brown corduroy jacket over a black turtleneck sweater and looked thrillingly bohemian. 'Name?' he asked and wrote the information on a card. Then he motioned towards the cash register near the door and turned to someone else.

'Jeez, you can't do anything right,' Beryl sighed when she heard what had happened. 'There aren't any jobs in life where you get to read books!'

Alice listened while her mother explained the world in a voice composed of pent-up howls and judgements. Beryl's eyes were a dazzling blue and as Alice glanced away from them she wondered if she herself were actually mentally retarded, in some way that was subtle enough to escape the notice of strangers, but profound enough for her mother to recognize. On her fingers Beryl was enumerating the bosses for whom she'd performed praiseworthy work in her youth. Full of courage and intelligence, Beryl had been the best waitress, the best cleaning woman. The best, the best.

The following afternoon Alice and Wendy met behind a revolving display of greetings cards that shielded them from Mr Fordham's gaze. The Easter cards had just been put out on a rack rotating like a magic lantern, filled with images of hope.

'We only did it once without the diaphragm,' Wendy said. The results of the test would be ready at the end of the day and Wendy was leaving early, but Alice had to work until the store closed because it was Friday night. She grasped Wendy's hand helplessly, knowing she could do nothing if a speck really was clinging to Wendy's womb. When Alice turned the corner and hurried up the front walk to the Greggs' house that night, she stepped around a large Harley Davidson motorcycle parked on the path. One of Billy's friends often jumped the sidewalk with his bike and left the mechanical beast in the yard when he visited.

'Hello, darling,' Mrs Gregg said. 'Here's my other daughter,' she joked, calling over her shoulder to her husband.

Wendy sat in the wooden chair by her window, leaning her arm on the window-ledge. Her body appeared artificially composed. 'The test was positive,' she said after Alice shut the bedroom door.

What good was the tenderness and protectiveness that flooded her now, Alice wondered. Emotion was so useless. 'What did Don say when you told him?' she asked.

'He says he's too young to get married,' Wendy said.

'I can't believe it,' Alice exclaimed.

'He said that before he used to tell me what would make me happy. Now he's telling me what he really feels,' Wendy went on in a wondering voice while tears ran out of the corners of her eyes, and she jumped up, combing her hair savagely, twisting it on to pink foam curlers. 'Don's dad says he'll kick him out of the house if he doesn't marry me,' she cried.

Alice and Wendy agreed Don was a monster who'd deceived them all along. Arthur Morel married his pregnant girlfriend unhesitatingly, Alice told Wendy who listened carefully. Don should be grateful to have a chance to marry Wendy!

'But he doesn't care,' Wendy whispered.

CHAPTER EIGHT

WHEN SHE LEFT WENDY'S, Alice was surprised to see Billy crouching in the dark adjusting some part of the motorcycle with a spanner. He pushed the heavy machine into the street and offered her a ride. Alice said yes even though she regarded the powerful bike uneasily and pictured herself lying in a ditch. Yet she was amazed she could even worry about the possibility of an accident when her friend was being punished and possibly destroyed by implacable biological forces.

'Put your feet there. Hold on to me,' Billy yelled, straddling the motorcycle and kicking violently at its side.

Roaring up the hill, Alice looked across the water at the lights of the city, while she wondered why Miriam and Clara hadn't become pregnant when they had sex with Paul in *Sons and Lovers*. Why Wendy? Alice and Billy shot around a corner, the motorcycle slanting towards the rushing pavement. Biology seemed inappropriate in the modern world, like a thunderclap over a city or a bear padding through a suburb. 'Lean into it,' Billy shouted. 'Don't fight it.'

At her house, Alice nodded wordlessly when Billy asked her to see a movie with him, her mind on the way blind sperm raced towards the egg lolling passively about in its fleshy chamber. What a terrible system, she grieved, a sort of evolutionary leftover completely unsuited to the life of the modern woman.

Wendy reported everything that Don said. He'd begun to reminisce about their first dates, recalling that he thought Wendy was funny and cute. Slouched beside him on the plastic seat of his parked car, Wendy listened. 'Remember when we went to Lighthouse Park, Wen?' he'd ask, his arms draped over the steering wheel. 'Remember when we went camping at Qualicum?' He didn't know what the word love meant any more, he told Wendy, and wasn't sure he'd ever known.

'What does THAT mean?' Alice asked.

Wendy leaned against the sink in the staff washroom at Woolworth's clicking the button up and down on the empty soap dispenser. Notices on the walls instructed employees not to linger.

'I think he wants me to go away to have the baby and give it up.'

'And then come back and be engaged to him?'

'Yes.' Wendy stared hopelessly at Alice.

Don met Wendy every night after work because he didn't want to go home for dinner at a table presided over by his angry father. During the day, Alice and Wendy sneaked up to the stockroom to mull over his incomprehensible opinions. The narrow aisles were dimly lit and on days when new shipments arrived, the air was pungent with chemical odours. When Alice told Wendy she had a date with Billy, her friend set down her stock basket, brimming with tiny boxes and tubes. The front of her smock was soiled from levering heavy baskets against her abdomen.

'Just don't let him take advantage of you, that's all,' Wendy said bitterly. 'He had sex with Linda MacIntyre and even told her he'd marry her, but afterwards he never talked to her again.'

Alice shifted slippery packages against her chest protectively.

'Then she came over to see him and he locked himself in the basement and got Mom to tell her he was out.'

On Friday, the early shift left Woolworth's at six o'clock and the parking spots in front of the store were occupied by husbands' and boyfriends' cars. Puzzling about Linda MacIntyre, Alice waited outside in her new skirt with a flower appliquéd on the front, its green stem twisting around the scalloped hem. She watched Wendy duck into Don's car and then Billy's voice called from the back seat of a dark, rumbling automobile that pulled up. When she bent to enter Alice tried not to be aware that there seemed to be something absurd about her own new garment and Billy's shaved, perfumed skin. She feared the idea of a date was better than the actual meeting where the quivering atmosphere Lawrence described, the ecstatic, silent communion, might not occur.

Pete, Billy's best friend, grinned from the driver's seat. He was a dark, corpulent man who combed his hair into a glossy pompadour reminiscent of Elvis and his sideburns were hairy flaps on his cheeks. He had a job at the airport where he inscribed messages in the air with flags and with him was his girlfriend, Debbie, a teller at the Bank of Montreal.

'Oh, baby,' Pete groaned when they stopped at a drive-in restaurant where waitresses wore short skirts. 'I can't help it,' he laughed, flinching from Debbie's reproving poke. 'It's human nature.'

Billy's lips pulled into a smile too and his shirt stretched across the hard muscles of his chest. Wendy said she had put her ear next to the heating vent in her room and heard disgusting things uttered by Billy and his friends in the basement, but Alice wondered if men were forced to produce such remarks and didn't believe them at all. When Pete started the motor, switching on the lights to signal the waitress to fetch the tray covered with crumpled bits of foil, Chubby Checker started to sing on the radio, and suddenly Debbie was a frenzy of activity, snapping her blonde head back and forth and jiggling her shoulders in time to the music.

'You should see her dance,' Pete yelled, pulling the car on to Georgia Street. 'She goes crazy!'

Debbie rolled down her window and slapped the roof of the car rhythmically.

'She gets me into trouble,' Pete roared. 'I can't take her to a club without getting into a fight.'

Alice glanced at Billy whose eyes were half-closed. 'Sounds like fun,' he declared.

Alice recognized Billy and Pete were of the same opinion as D. H. Lawrence about the necessity for physical contest between men; afterwards these men felt bonded in a mystical way. At the theatre, she and Debbie clicked up the steps ahead of the men, ascending the sweeping staircase and drifting into the palatial washroom where Debbie confided that her family was opposed to Pete because he was a Protestant. 'What are you?' she asked. She was a tiny woman, beautifully groomed and clothed in palest blue wool. In her imagination, Alice could hear the question expanding. 'I'm a devotee of Lawrence,' she might have said in an offhand, sophisticated voice. But instead she just shrugged and traced her lips with lipstick. She figured it was still possible for the mood of the evening to change, for detachment to be carried away in a flood of feeling. Everything would be different if that happened.

Seated in the dark theatre, they all stared straight ahead while activity took place sideways; hands scrabbled across armrests and cartons of popcorn slid past. At the edge of Alice's vision she saw Billy lift a piece of popcorn to his mouth while a knife on the screen flashed towards a woman's abdomen. Alice wished she were the kind of girl who'd draw moody poets towards her, dazzling them with her allure; however, she knew this would never happen unless she were worthy, possessed of extraordinary magnificence, gleaming with female vitality. Might Billy be the one to release her into this sort of state, the true womanhood Lawrence reverenced?

CHAPTER NINE

THE NIGHT-SCHOOL TEACHER had just posed a question not one student could answer, a question that transfixed Alice with the boldness of its penetration and the splendour of its conception. This was the sort of question real intellectuals asked, she thought, delighted.

'What is a novel?'

Alice saw instantly how superficial her thinking was, how she accepted crude existence without a query. She'd wandered casually into the class, the first student to appear, eyeing the dusty blackboard, the bulletin board with its notices, and the classroom walls that brought back memories of her own high-school years when teachers handed out scraps of easily lost paper while droning on about the irrelevant topics that seemed to preoccupy them. The air had seemed to shimmer with adolescent lamentation and rage. With a novel propped under her desk at the back of the class, Alice had read hypnotically throughout grades eight and nine but had drifted out in the tenth.

'Is a book just a toy? Is reading a novel merely an entertaining pastime?' the teacher demanded, his dark brown hair touching the collar of his turtleneck sweater at the back. His name was James Chant and when he asked these questions his wiry beard lifted up aggressively.

'A novel is a thought-adventure in which we journey through the wilderness seeking our sacred home. A book is like life in that there are pillars of cloud and fire aplenty as well as golden calves. Which will you follow? Truth or lies? That which leads to discovery or that which leads to unconsciousness. Reality or illusion?

'Man's long, yearning venture into consciousness involves the whole man, not only his mind and spirit but his blood. His blood thinks and makes conclusions that are more powerful and true than any mind trick. Logic is far too crude and coarse to make the subtle distinctions demanded by life.'

Alice knew literature was more real than ordinary life, more vivid and interesting. She stared bewitched at the teacher's delicate lower lip that curved in a crescent within his beard.

'We must recognize our blood-being,' the teacher insisted, throwing back his head like a nervous horse. 'The important question is not the formal one of whether a work of fiction is a novel or novella – what I want you to ask yourselves is whether a work is a pillar of fire or a seductive, lying *ignis fatuus*.'

The teacher paced back and forth at the front of the room while his tender, boyish ears flushed with emotion. 'It shouldn't take people forty years to find their way out of a wilderness,' he cried. 'That's why we're going to concentrate on the novels of David Herbert Lawrence, starting, in the next class, with *Sons and Lovers*.'

Alice thought she might faint.

Mr Chant rattled a nub of chalk in his palm. 'Lawrence was a man who was the son of a miner and all his life he sought to follow the pillar of fire. He defied the class system by becoming a writer, his society by marrying a divorced woman and the frightened, filthy ideas of his generation by letting the force of God and truth fill him. He was a great writer and we'll see whether or not you show yourselves worthy of him.'

Here the teacher tossed the chalk up in the air and caught it with an overhand swoop. 'I have faith in you,' he said cheerfully, gazing at the class who regarded him with a range of puzzled, even stupefied, expressions. 'So have that book read by next week, will you?'

A woman in a blue cardigan shot her hand up and asked anxiously where such a book could be obtained, her face twisted into a worried grimace. Alice was possessed by a desire to annihilate her own false, superficial self and embrace this teacher's uplifting vision. One could buy it at Duthie Books, the teacher said, or at second-hand bookshops near the university.

'I'm a Lawrence scholar,' the teacher announced, his intense face lit with his subject. Alice imagined him in a stone, academic building, bent over books, his face pale with study, and then afterwards, dressed in something dark with a scarf thrown over his shoulder sitting in a bohemian café filled with students conversing about mysteries.

At her mother's, seeing herself nobly following a column of fire while others stumbled into error and darkness, Alice swept past Beryl. 'What's with her?' Beryl mocked, staring at the ceiling and waddling down the hall in imitation of Alice's exaltation.

CHAPTER TEN

ALICE TRIED ON a push-up bra. The cups were white lace, puffed with a thin layer of foam rubber underneath and she regarded her pushed-up breasts in the department store mirror while they lay on the foam shells like innocent sea creatures. Above them her face was pale and concerned. Her familiar cotton brassiere lay in a twisted heap on the fitting-room floor while she reached up experimentally and fiddled with her hair, thinking it should be more frivolous, have curls and waves perhaps, to be compatible with such daring underwear.

Don had agreed to marry Wendy, so now Alice would have to pace up the aisle of the church too, clad in a turquoise Maid of Honour's dress. Underneath she'd wear the kind of lingerie she'd admired when she'd studied the Eaton's catalogues as a child.

'You said yes?' Alice had asked her friend, amazed. After all, hadn't Wendy given examples of Don's behaviour that proved he was irredeemably cruel, selfish, immature and untrustworthy?

Wendy had nodded briskly, her mind now on the wedding.

In her bedroom, Alice tucked the new underwear into a dresser drawer.

'Get rid of all this crap,' Beryl ordered, motioning towards the volumes on the floor beside Alice's bed. 'It's a bloody fire hazard in here.'

'Actually, I have to buy more books for that course I'm taking.'

'Actually,' Beryl mimicked, 'you're getting to be a weirdo. A crutch. That's what Maggie said all this reading you do is. You can't face reality.'

In a North Vancouver hotel, Alice and Wendy examined brochures depicting possible meals for the reception. 'Everyone's going to have a hot roll,' Wendy announced in her definite voice when she signed the agreement. She'd been saving for the wedding ever since she and Don had picked out her engagement ring with its tiny diamond. Alice trailed after her friend, carrying packages and bags, marvelling at the way Wendy was creating a proper wedding out of nothing.

Seated on a padded banquette in a bridal salon fitting room, Alice observed Wendy standing radiant while a saleslady crouched at her feet, marking the hem of a white wedding dress with pins.

Wendy smiled, her lips pearly with the new shade of lipstick she'd just put out on her counter that week. Then with a queenly gesture she dropped the dress over the arms of the waiting saleslady who bore it reverently away.

When it was time for the real thing, Wendy floated down the aisle taking the small steps the minister had demonstrated during rehearsals, while her father, listing slightly as he held on to her arm, led her to the altar where Don waited. Alice stared down at her pointed, turquoise satin shoes hearing Wendy and Don pronounce terrible vows, FORSAKING ALL OTHERS.

Onlookers gazed upon the couple approvingly, and after the ceremony when Alice would talk to her friend, she'd be speaking to Don's wife, a woman who could breathe the words, 'my husband'. Don was lucky he'd caught such a soft, fresh wife, Alice thought; the ceremony was short for an act of such consequence.

Alice trooped into the reception hall with the rest of the wedding party, but it reminded her of the kind of place where people set up cots after a disaster. Hotel staff had arranged tables in the barren space and covered the U-shape with white cloths, like a makeshift altar. After the guests had settled themselves, waitresses rushed into the room carrying plates of cold meat, each one a perfect copy of the prototype illustrated in the coloured folder Alice and Wendy had seen – a slice of pale, damp chicken folded over a round of ham loaf beside a spoonful of mayonnaised vegetables decorated with a gherkin.

Her veil thrown back in a frothy puff, Wendy smiled while Don sat beside her, grinning wildly, eyes shining at male relatives who shouted encouraging remarks. Wendy's waist was tiny; underneath the peau de soie of her wedding dress she was girdled by a tube of thick, pink rubber punched with tiny holes.

After the plates were cleared away, the staff pushed tables against the wall and Don's two sisters sat together and watched the dancing while they called out threats and warnings to their children who played tag under the tables. The sisters, Marilyn and Carolyn, wore lace sheath dresses and their blonde hair was teased into formal puffs and cones. Their husbands stood in the corner, telling jokes and drinking from flasks hidden inside their jackets.

Alice moved her slick stockinged legs back and forth in a dance step while she clung to Billy who was Don's best man. It was as if she was the survivor of a terrible accident, still wearing her cloudy nylon dress despite its inappropriate festivity. Billy drew her over to a corner and sucked at the mickey of whisky he carried in his pocket, while Alice tried not to recall that he Fletcherized his food, chewing each bite fifty times so all nutrients would be absorbed by his body.

'I guess I might get married next,' he announced despondently. 'I'm older than Wendy.' He slid his fingers back and forth on Alice's shoulder. 'Even Pete's talking about it. In a couple of years, we'll all be hitched up.' His hand moved under the nylon strap of the dress that had a tiny loop sewn inside into which she'd threaded the strap of the French brassiere.

Alice saw people dancing with ugly energy while music, too thin to fill the large, blank room, came from the record-player. She only half-listened to Billy's conversation, conscious of his voice recounting histories of friends who were now engaged, conjuring up images of damp, cold cribs pushed into future back bedrooms, mashed teething biscuits on rugs and other miseries, none greater than the fact that this would go on, with minor variations, until death.

Though she didn't want to stand frozen in hopeless observation, like someone forced to watch an appalling event against her will, her limbs were heavy, scarcely alive. Her lips felt paralysed as well, disconnected, as if they were just two coloured pieces of paper. She used to fall into the same mute torpor as a child when Beryl whirled above, arms churning the air in ecstasies of rage. Alice was chagrined to find her adult self now comatose at the edge of the dance floor at her best friend's wedding.

She made herself join the group of unmarried women who leapt up to catch the flowers Wendy tossed in their direction. She was embarrassed to be observed in such a humiliating activity and she was also ashamed that her self-consciousness prevented her from making a serious attempt to grasp the dark roses that sailed over her head. D. H. Lawrence despised self-consciousness.

'I tried to aim the flowers in your direction,' Wendy whispered to Alice as they embraced.

Alice smiled resolutely and waved with the others as she watched her friend leave.

CHAPTER ELEVEN

ALICE WAS CERTAIN the tension in her teacher's face and body was evidence of a flood of passion and ideas. Reading aloud from the novel in a resonant voice, he leaned over the desk, standing with arms stiff, hands clenching the edges of the desk's surface. Then, flipping the book shut, he stood back and gazed challengingly at the class, crossing his arms loosely over his chest and clasping his upper arms with hands that were, surprisingly, not refined or artistic; in fact, their heavy shape was faintly brutal. Alice decided to edit this characteristic from the teacher's image.

'Well,' Mr Chant asked, 'what's the book about?' There was a faint vertical crease between his eyebrows.

'Love?' someone in the class ventured.

'But who was in love with whom?' he challenged. 'Did Paul really love Miriam or Clara as a man must to be fully alive?'

The students shuffled with embarrassment but Alice sat up straight in her chair. In the harsh overhead light she could see the teacher's eyes were not plain brown, but were golden near the edges of the iris. She felt guilty of not completely understanding why Mrs Morel was finally so destructive. When Alice heard Mrs Morel's voice saying the words 'my son', weak tears filled her eyes.

'Wasn't he held in check by the terrible love of his mother?' Mr Chant prompted.

'Well, at least he really loved *her*,' a woman said. There were only two men in the class.

'He did kill her,' Mr Chant replied.

'That was MERCY!' the students called out.

'Yes, but to whom?' Mr Chant asked. 'Paul Morel freed

· 57 ·

himself by getting rid of a mother whose love had become a prison. She was *his* cancer, if you like, clinging crablike to him with a grip he had to break to be a man.' The teacher walked back and forth in front of the class like a prophet, while his students cried out distressed objections and Alice studied his reflection in the window. It was clear he was isolated by his superiority, the fluidity and grandeur of his ideas. His collar was frayed and she thought the loose threads were evidence of his high ideals; this was not a man who'd ponder about his appearance the way she did, fretting over the colour of a sweater, something utterly unimportant compared to infinite values.

The teacher waved away the class's comments. 'We need to inhabit what Lawrence called "the realm of calm delight . . . the other kingdom of bliss in which a man and woman mix and mingle and yet remain single in contradistinction. This kind of love is the perfect heartbeat of life, systole and diastole" – – sacred and profane: the most complete passion possible. Paul Morel yearned towards healing conjunction with a woman, but he also sensed that he must keep himself utterly separate, which meant a new transcendent configuration had to blossom. However, first the implacable mother had to be killed. Her death was creative in providing earth from which his new life sprung.' Mr Chant stared broodingly around the room. 'We are all flowers incipient with blossom,' he finished.

Alice followed the others out into the hall during the break where they stood in little groups and smoked cigarettes, dropping the ashes into makeshift ashtrays, all except the real-estate agent who produced a portable metal ashtray decorated with a mound of pearls.

'Why are you here?' a voice asked.

Alice had noticed the speaker whose chopped hair was dyed a shocking black and held away from her face by two pink, plastic barrettes. She was a thin woman of about thirty-five and she bent forward as Alice spoke.

'What? I can't hear you,' the woman said with annoyance. In soft, waxy hands she held a clear plastic handbag fastened with a pink flowered clasp. With frantic intensity she told Alice she'd spent six months in Riverview Clinic and now had to obtain regular shots of some calming drug from her own doctor. Her social worker had advised a night-school course. Alice couldn't prevent herself from studying the contents of the woman's handbag. Horrid things lay within the clear envelope.

After the break, Mr Chant explained that the whole question of profound love was set against the evil, deadening background of industrialism which killed the human being, body, soul and spirit. What kind of people would Lawrence write about now if he wanted to depict meagre urban lives? the teacher wondered.

'Someone working in Woolworth's?' Alice ventured.

'A chain of stores that epitomizes bad taste, shoddiness and dehumanization,' Mr Chant agreed.

'I work there,' Alice announced provocatively.

The teacher ran his hand through his hair. 'The whole chain is a monument to death.'

Enthralled, Alice gazed at him.

When the class was over the students wandered out but Mr Chant stopped Alice. 'I'm having a party Saturday night,' he said. 'Would you like to come?' He picked up his jacket from the back of the chair and slung it over his shoulder.

The teacher understood perfectly what it was like to work at Woolworth's, Alice thought worshipfully, recalling the beauty and sternness of his ideas as she walked home with the spring night around her, quiet and expectant, fragrant with clipped lawns.

Wendy invited Alice to the little suite she and Don had rented in the east end of the city. Their furnished apartment was on the top floor of a quiet house where the landlord lived downstairs, and on Saturday nights Alice would carry her nightgown in her purse and sleep over at Wendy's. Now that she was safely married, Wendy wore maternity smocks and had quit work. Alice told Wendy and Don about the novel course, but Wendy said it sounded too much like school.

'It's not,' Alice responded. 'It's like sitting up late at night discussing things.'

Wendy intended to take a class from the public health nurse

who taught pregnant women to relax and breathe deeply. All pain in childbirth was caused by fear, Wendy's doctor said. This had been discovered by a medical man who figured pain resulted from wrong thinking and tension. If women would not co-operate, science was still willing to help by administering anaesthetic gas during the birth. Wendy planned to ask for this soporific as soon as she reached the hospital. Alice, Wendy and Don sat in the kitchen and gossiped while they ate snacks Wendy fashioned out of toast, ketchup, cheese and green pepper. Don wasn't as bad as she'd once thought, Alice decided; in fact, her visits were like a girls' pyjama party. She slept in a single bed in the same room as her friends.

One Sunday morning Wendy rose first, complaining that Alice and Don were lazy. From their respective beds they smiled up at her. 'Do you want pancakes?' Wendy demanded, standing with her hand on one hip. 'Get dressed then,' she ordered. Her movements were always energetic and she often waved someone away while she took over a situation or solved a problem. She routinely fixed Don's car, leaning under the hood and fiddling with various parts of the engine.

'I'm going out to get butter,' she announced and Alice and Don heard her footsteps as she marched down the long back staircase, then the sound of the engine as she started the car.

Alice folded her arms under her head and planned how she would swiftly get out of bed in one motion.

'Are you lonely over there?' Don asked.

'No,' Alice said.

'Here I come,' he sang out, leaping across the space between them. His white body in blue underpants flashed through the air and imprisoned Alice in a cage of arms and legs. When she pushed against him he was immovable, like a spidery insect clamping its prey in a digestive embrace. Don mashed his hand over her mouth as she kicked and thrashed under him. 'Shut up. Someone will hear you.' He laughed and thrust his hand under her nightgown, his light blue eyes shining with excitement. His skin smelled like mushrooms. Alice ground her teeth against the palm he clasped over her mouth and suddenly he curled on the side of the bed, clutching his wounded hand.

'You crazy bitch,' he screamed.

She ran to the bathroom and locked the door, turning on the shower and standing under the spray while water ran into her mouth, but she could still taste Don's flesh. When his pregnant wife was out innocently buying butter to give him a breakfast treat, Don had flown through the air and wrapped his limbs around her best friend. How could he? Alice scrubbed at herself with a washcloth.

'You washed your hair?' Wendy asked Alice. She'd set the table neatly with matching melmac plates and paper napkins. With a flourish, she clapped a hot platter of steaming pancakes on to the centre of the table and sat down, her cheeks rosy from the heat of the stove.

Alice was aware of the aggressive slouch of Don's body and the way he placed his arm on the table so she had to move her plate. He shovelled portions into his mouth, eating silently like a machine while Wendy chatted happily. The important thing was that Wendy must never know, Alice thought.

Her silence was a secret gift to her friend.

CHAPTER TWELVE

THE TELEVISION SET was broken. At first the picture rolled for a moment and then bands of black began floating rapidly across the screen in ceaseless motion. Beryl squatted in her red chair and brooded, glancing at Alice who was bent over a book. Wet, hissing cars plunged through the downpour outside. Now that the television's voice was quiet the house was thick with silence, punctuated by occasional moans from shifting floorboards and surges of the refrigerator's motor. Beryl waited nervously for the repairman and when the phone rang she grabbed it.

'Maybe,' she crooned suggestively into the receiver. 'That depends on who's calling, doesn't it?' She wriggled roguishly and rolled her eyes. Alice took the call, turning her head away and listened to Billy inviting her to go out, but she was determined to go alone to her teacher's party that night, so she settled on a date later in the week with Billy.

Alice thought about this new development while she stood at the door of an old, wooden rooming house on Thurlow near Robson, listening to the sounds of James's party coming from the upper floor. Billy was almost as beautiful as Wendy but so far Alice had not yet noticed herself feeling anything Laurentian when she was with him. Hoping to appear indistinguishable from the teacher's other guests, Alice had drawn black lines around her eyes to suggest sophistication, but now she feared the pencilled line was thicker on one side so her left eye looked aggressive and sluttish. She worried that her dress was all wrong too, pale blue cotton with a gathered skirt. Despite this, she pushed open the door and made her way up a narrow, dusty staircase leading to a landing where she could hear strange and undanceable music she was sure must be jazz. She felt she was ascending to an extraordinary domain, like walking into a novel, so she wasn't surprised when a stranger stuck his head out of an open door and pulled her in.

'The booze is in the kitchen,' he announced as he led her through a dark vestibule into a bright room where light slanted off enamel surfaces. Everything was unfamiliar and dreamlike and Alice reached out like a somnambulist for the glass of wine the man handed her. He was a tall man with sandy hair and he stood beside a kitchen table covered with bottles and spilled wine.

'I'm Gordon, by the way. Who are you?'

Alice thought he said, 'I'm gorgon.'

'Do you know James?' Gordon asked, swilling his wine around in the clear plastic cup and holding it up to the light.

'He's my teacher.'

'That dog!' Gordon peered at her. 'How old are you, anyway?'

'Nineteen,' Alice cried. Did he think she was a child? She lifted her glass and gulped a large mouthful of dark, bitter wine. Gordon's large face loomed above her. 'Well, you don't look it,' he said. 'Watch out for James. He seduces young girls.'

Alice was amazed Gordon could be so wrong. Mr Chant had the same moral views as D. H. Lawrence and was concerned with eternal values.

'Who does?' A woman in a black leotard pranced into the kitchen.

'James,' Gordon answered.

'How lovely!' the woman exclaimed, opening the refrigerator and taking out a beer. 'Do you think he'll seduce me?' She pulled off the cap and left, saluting them with the bottle.

Gordon told Alice he'd been in university but had quit when he decided to be a folk singer. James rented the apartment cheaply from the city and sublet the back bedroom to Gordon. 'Want to see it?' he inquired.

'No, thank you.'

'No one ever does,' Gordon said sadly. 'Perhaps no one ever will because the city's going to demolish this row of houses some day and we may have to get out fast.'

'Gordon! Gordon!' Two women rushed into the kitchen and led him, protesting, to the living room. Alice grasped her drink and followed.

A few candles burned in squat, raffia-covered wine bottles in the dark room where guests lounged on an old sofa or on the floor. A record-player was set on a low bookcase constructed of bricks and pieces of raw lumber, while the walls were decorated with large, dramatic posters depicting Paris, London and Vienna. The women wore dark, serious clothing and held their bodies in careless and unusual positions. Alice could see at once that her own pastel sundress looked absurd, exactly like a milkmaid's costume. The two women were still tending Gordon, pushing him on to the couch, handing him a guitar and turning off the record. In a high tenor voice Gordon began to sing about a dying maiden, but then Alice caught sight of James Chant cross-legged on the floor, his face illuminated from beneath by the candle set in front of him.

'*Willow, willow,*' Gordon sang, face contorted and eyes closed.

'Alice,' James called out, beckoning, and she picked her way over people's outstretched limbs towards him. 'I'm glad you could come,' he said, standing up when she reached him, his beard glittering in the light. Alice examined his expression carefully to see if she could detect mockery but there seemed to be genuine pleasure in his face. 'Sit down,' he invited and, after Alice settled the folds of her skirt around her legs beside him on the floor, he introduced her to the woman at his side.

She was called Mara and Alice saw she had lips that appeared wonderfully pouting and thick blonde hair that was heavy and beautiful like a princess. Her nose was very straight and the voice in which she greeted Alice was assured, full of the cadences of Kerrisdale. Gordon finished his song and someone put on another record.

'I love Thelonius Monk,' Mara exclaimed and they listened for a moment without talking. 'So many twists,' she commented. 'What do you do, Alice?' she asked after a silence.

'I'm a salesgirl at Woolworth's.'

'How INTERESTING!' Mara cried, clapping her hands

together. 'You are absolutely the first person I've met who has ever given that answer.'

Alice glanced at James who was watching them both.

'I love the windows they do and the amusing signs.' Mara paused. 'You know – like: "Men! Try our bargain pyjamas!" '

Alice stared at the dark bits at the bottom of her cup.

'A sort of bad taste emporium!' Mara laughed. 'I adore the naïveté of those messages.'

Alice opened her white patent leather purse and took a cigarette from an open packet which had spilled bits of tobacco into the creases of the lining. This was just like D. H. Lawrence: two women, one urban and one rural, with an onlooking man. Perhaps she wasn't really rural but she did live in North Vancouver.

James spoke lazily, leaning back on one elbow. 'Alice is my star student.'

'In your night-school class? How dedicated!' Mara turned the silver ring on her finger. 'I can only take afternoon classes because even mornings are out for me. I just don't have the right metabolism for it.'

'Mara thinks laziness is a medical condition,' James joked.

'That's not fair!' Mara smiled. 'I'm only in third year. I'm not an exalted grad student like you, James.'

'Last year she was in Art History,' James said. 'This year she's in English. It's taken her four years to get to third year.'

Mara laughed. '"Consistency is the hobgoblin of little minds."'

'Foolish consistency,' James corrected.

'I hope you like Lawrence,' Mara said suddenly, turning to Alice. 'That's what James is doing his doctorate on.'

'What's a doctorate?' Alice inquired.

Mara giggled and looked at James. 'A Ph.D.,' she said, smiling. 'When you have a Ph.D. you get a job as a professor, don't you James?'

Alice listened to Mara's drawling voice describing a recent evening she'd spent at the Little Heidelberg Café, a place frequented by artists. The man across from Alice was talking about Camus and the woman leaning against him gazed soulfully at her feet wound with thongs and straps. The man's feet were similarly clad, only with thicker, sturdier straps as if his heavier, male feet needed stronger bonds. The woman murmured something and fingered her sandal. 'I'd say you're guilty of *mauvaise foi*,' she taunted. The man's longish hair fell into his eyes and he flung it back.

Next to this couple sat an extraordinarily thin man with grey hair who moved his head from side to side in time with the music and put a cigarette to his lips, all without opening his eyes. James said this was Professor Wilson who taught poetry at the university. Someone's wine spilled, surging out suddenly in a rivulet on to the dusty rug and a woman in a dark green jumper leapt up.

'Never mind,' James called out but the woman took no notice, rushing to the kitchen and returning with a rag which she rubbed determinedly on the dark spot. A male hand reached out and patted her rump, then someone rapped for attention and Alice saw a tall woman wearing a shapeless garment standing at one end of the room. She was about thirty, thin, with carelessly cut brown hair and she held a sheaf of typed pages from which she began to read, beating her left hand rhythmically in the air while the strand of coffee beans she wore swung back and forth.

'Phillipa Kirke,' James whispered, putting his hand on Alice's shoulder. After he took his hand away she could feel the warm weight of his fingers on her skin. The woman read a long poem and Alice sat carefully and respectfully still. Phillipa Kirke's face was pale and two creases ran from the sides of her nose towards her mouth. Her stiff, nervous shoulders were held high as she gripped the pages of poetry.

'Come and meet her!' James invited Alice when the poetess had finished and Alice imagined she was being pulled through one of those hallucinatory tunnels in amusement parks where extraordinary tableaux are successively revealed.

'This is Alice,' James announced, pushing her towards Phillipa. 'The flower in the desert of my night-school class.'

Phillipa laughed a long, almost hysterical peal and James giggled too, although Alice considered the shocking high-pitched sound to be an aberration in his case because his natural mien was sensitive and serious. The poet's face was very long and noble with its aristocratic nose and lips, Alice thought. In her large hands the woman held a smouldering cigar which she sucked nonchalantly.

'I suppose you're a Lawrence devotee like your teacher?' Phillipa asked in a carrying voice.

Alice observed such tones were usual for intellectual women. At Woolworth's the women had higher, strained voices that gained power only by increasing in sharpness or volume, but the women at the party had access to richness and resonance of tone as well as perfection of pronunciation.

'He was a genius of course but perhaps just a little fanatical,' Phillipa commented.

'Really, Phillipa,' James said impatiently. 'How can somebody be a little fanatical?'

Alice watched the secret, intimate tightening of Phillipa's face. Intellectuals engaged each other in a mutual progression towards truth, free of pettiness. They didn't have to translate thoughts and feelings into acceptable forms to please their listeners. In this world Alice would be allowed to speak fully about anything. She was astounded at the miraculous turning of fate that had brought her here. When James walked her down the long flight of stairs and stood with her in the street for a moment she took it as a promise of continuity.

CHAPTER THIRTEEN

BERYL WAITED in the living room.

'Now don't get upset,' she warned. 'I've got something to tell you.' She paused dramatically and laid one hand on her breast.

'What's wrong?' Alice gripped the doorway.

'Goldie's in the hospital,' Beryl said. 'He had a heart attack but it was mild – nothing to worry or get excited about.'

Alice envisioned Mr Goldman's heart squeezing painfully in his chest like a crushed valentine.

'He fell in the laundromat and one of the women called an ambulance,' Beryl said, smoking rapidly, her eyebrows pulled together. 'They called his brother-in-law, Ben, and he phoned me tonight.' Beryl raised her chin bravely. 'Maggie said the most important thing to remember is that I have to take care of myself.'

'Did you talk to the doctor?'

'See? You're getting all worked up,' Beryl said. 'How can I talk to the doctor? That's Ben's job!' She twisted her empty cigarette packet and pulled the seal off another one.

In bed Alice held the covers up to her neck, imagining Mr Goldman's blood rushing through the dark tunnels of his body. She hated biological systems with all those fragile quivering interiors. When she was a girl she'd had a doll made of spongy stuff and she wanted to think people were composed of the same consistent, sturdy, uncomplicated material. The idea that Mr Goldman was not invulnerable, but was made up of delicate interconnecting parts and that all these components were formed of flesh, was just more evidence of how flawed the universe really was.

She awoke to the sound of the television and knew David

was sitting in his pyjamas watching *The Three Stooges*. The repairman had replaced a tube in the set, but Beryl was sure his fiddling had distorted the picture so she could see ghostly, semivisible channels underneath the show she was watching. This was a common practice, she said; repairmen guaranteed their future work by disconnecting wires and unscrewing tubes.

'Leave me alone,' David squealed when Alice poked him with her toe, but his eyes didn't move from the television screen.

A fine rain was falling on to the yard which was green and tangled like a witch's garden. Alice made toast for David, scraping the margarine quickly across the bread before it soaked in. Then she set the plate on the floor in front of the child and he reached out his hand without looking.

Bearing a tray full of invalid dishes before her like a religious offering, Alice saw herself gliding down the hallway towards Mr Goldman's bed where he'd be ruddy from sun that would stream through open windows. She heard a moan from her mother's room and opened the door to a heavy smell of dampness and dirt.

'What time is it?' Beryl asked in a thick, distorted voice.

'Almost noon.'

'Goldie sure didn't think of my nerves when he had that heart attack, let me tell you,' Beryl groaned.

Alice yanked the stiff dun-coloured blind and pale light illuminated the room where her mother lay folded under the blankets. There was a thick layer of dust on the vanity, and the night table held two empty cups, a full ashtray, a safety pin, a bit of string and a hairbrush spraying hairy tentacles. Beryl pulled herself up slowly, lighting a cigarette.

'Ben's got everything worked out so Goldie won't get too tired,' she said. 'I go at two o'clock, someone else goes at two-thirty. Like that.'

'Have you met Ben?'

'Are you kidding? They're too hoity-toity! I saw Goldie's sister once, not the one that was married to Ben. Another one. She's in Florida or someplace now. Miriam, her name was. She says to me, "Beryl you made my brother less lonely." I met her at the laundromat and Goldie just sat there staring straight ahead like a corpse. You know how he is. Quiet. Anyways, I showed her a picture of David, and she said he looked exactly like her grandfather.'

'Maybe we'll meet Ben today,' Alice said, seeing their two families merging, with religious differences unimportant in the crisis.

'Forget about WE,' Beryl cried. 'I'M the only one that's going. You'll stay here and look after David.'

'Why can't I go?'

'Because you weren't invited, that's why. Only people who are close get to go. Like family. Someone's got to take care of David, too. Jeez, don't start getting on my nerves first thing in the morning.' Beryl scratched her scalp vigorously.

'I'm usually at work on Saturdays. I hardly ever get a Saturday off. What would you do if I were at work?' Alice cried.

'Just don't bug me.' Beryl sat on the side of the bed leaning forward, looking at the floor. 'I don't even know what I'm going to wear.' She staggered over and pushed at the hangers in her closet.

Alice peered out the window into the space between her mother's house and the neighbour's, noticing a mound of sodden grass clippings and a broken chair.

'Do you have any stockings?' Beryl crouched on the floor inside her closet, pulling out shoes. 'I got to look good. Do you think I should wear my fur?'

'No!' The thin strip had small animal heads at one end, tails at the other and a cluster of sharp claws.

When she returned from the hospital, Beryl dragged off her jacket and skirt. 'I'm glad that's over,' she exclaimed, standing in her nylon blouse and slip.

'How was he?'

'Pale. The nurse says Goldie's not supposed to smoke any more cigars. She even made me put out my cigarette. A real old battleaxe.' Beryl snapped the dial on the television. Her suit lay on the floor where it had fallen.

'Is my dad dead?' David asked, grimacing nervously.

'Don't be nuts,' Beryl answered.

Alice picked up the ashtrays and carried them to the kitchen where she opened the dark cupboard under the sink and dumped the butts and ashes into the brown paper garbage bag. Condensation ran down the back window, obscuring her view.

'Put the kettle on,' Beryl called from the living room.

When she handed Beryl her tea, her mother was already on the phone to Maggie. Alice set down the mug and walked out the door.

'Hey! Housework!' she heard her mother call, but she was down the path by then.

Mr Goldman's visitors turned around slowly and looked at her when she entered the room. They were seated at the bedside, quietly watching Mr Goldman who lay against the white pillows, his face drawn and grey like an old, sick man. One of the men held a book in his hand and wore a black yarmulke on his thin hair.

'Sorry to interrupt,' she burst out, seeing the scene as if projected on a tiny screen, herself in her new pearlized shoes and her pink dress, tottering in the doorway while the faces of Mr Goldman's relatives gazed mildly in her direction.

'I just stopped by to see Mr Goldman,' she explained.

The man in the yarmulke stood up and steered her into the shining hallway outside the door. 'Mr Goldman needs to rest,' he whispered. 'Thank you very much for coming.'

'I'm Alice,' she said.

'I'll tell him.' The man nodded politely.

She hurried out of the hospital, her throat burning. She was not a member of Mr Goldman's true family with the right to sit in the little group gazing at his face, calling his soul back from death. She kept her eyes open very wide, her body watered with internal, invisible weeping. Love was a terrible thing to offer when unwanted and it was kinder to resist any display of burdensome affection for a man who should have no stress on his heart.

CHAPTER FOURTEEN

ALICE HESITATED for a moment, peering through the steamy, lit window of the Little Heidelberg Café. At her teacher's party she'd listened like an ethnographer seeking clues to another culture, and now she opened the door and stepped inside this restaurant where there might be poets, her arms cradling library books and her mind agitated with the conversations that might possibly begin. She was aware of entering sudden warmth, the fragrance of spiced food and the sound of clashing cutlery. At the back corner was a woman with sorrowful eyes who shouted orders in German to someone in the kitchen. There were no empty tables.

As Alice lingered in the doorway, a man looked up from the book he was reading and motioned her to the unoccupied chair beside his own. She seated herself quickly, examining him for signs of bohemian qualities, but found nothing to encourage her except his upper lip which was sensually curved. Other than that, his face appeared battered and his dark blond hair was brushed back conventionally. His book had a French title, Alice saw, busy arranging her own volumes. She didn't notice for a moment that the man sat in a wheelchair.

He introduced himself formally as Michael Halek, adding that he was doing a postdoc in History, but Alice was determined not to be disappointed at this information which did not necessarily mean the man was mired down with boring facts and things. Smoking a cigarette with confident gestures, she announced she read nothing but fiction.

A waiter in black trousers and a white shirt presented her with a menu and she gazed at her hand moving back and forth as she spoke, seeing thin vapour drifting up in eddies from her cigarette, imagining that Mr Chant himself might rush in. The history professor seemed sympathetic, as if her predilection for literature were an affliction or vice, but she explained how life was mediated by literature, how its radiance could lift the soul from the brute level.

Snapping open her menu, she puzzled over a list of unfamiliar, Germanic dishes she feared might be curiously shaped and would require the manipulation of strange implements in order to be consumed.

'History,' said her companion, holding his knife and fork in the European manner, 'is the study of sad and chaotic human events.' The past gripped the present inexorably. That much was certain.

This was a depressing point of view that didn't take into account a person's true nature and ability, Alice thought. It was simply unacceptable to think that anonymous, overwhelming forces operated so unfairly. After all, this was the modern world. Magazines were stuffed with optimistic articles about what science had and would discover, how the tedium of work and the suffering of disease would soon be curiosities.

'An ahistorical view,' Michael said, grasping his fork like a prong and spearing a piece of potato. He said he was born in Montreal but his parents came from Bohemia, a part of Czechoslovakia.

'Bohemia,' she exclaimed. 'Really?' She had no idea such a place actually existed. She could feel the motion of the air as the door opened and closed like a gentle bellows when people came and went. All the while her senses were alert to the possibility of James Chant's arrival, but she lingered at the small table with Michael while the waiter refilled their cups.

No, she wasn't a university student, Alice said in answer to Michael's query, adding she was educating herself independently; a statement she savoured as she said it, thinking herself a rather dashing person. She'd first read a volume of fairy tales kept at her aunt's house. This woman had taken care of her for a few years when Beryl had been involved with a Norwegian sailor. He couldn't cope with the way Alice was always present in Beryl's rented room, sleeping in the only bed and awakening at inappropriate moments.

One day, without the sailor, Beryl had loomed in the doorway and had dragged her away from Aunt Mavis and the fairy tale books. 'That bitch,' Beryl fumed, her furious breath gusting out into the cold air, while Alice had trotted along beside her, the buckles on her boots jingling. Beryl had heard that Mavis was critical of the state of Alice's hair and ears when she'd been brought to her and a row had ensued that had never been resolved.

'I read legends as a child,' Alice explained to Michael, leaving out the part about Mavis and Beryl. 'And then short stories and poetry.' *The Book of Knowledge* Mr Goldman had brought home consisted of a set of heavy volumes with thin, shiny pages and dark blue, faded covers. She used to open them in her bedroom and whisper Shelley's poetry aloud, weeping. Now she laughed at the naïve girl she'd been, but the memory of Mr Goldman suffused her body with grief.

She'd been reading D. H. Lawrence, she told Michael. 'I'm taking a course from a wonderful teacher. He said we had to trace the development of our poetic so I've been thinking about my literary background.' Michael nodded politely while Alice remembered the smell and shape of her favourite books, picturing her hands caressing the spines and turning the pages with careful fingers.

Though unmoved by literature, Beryl was ravished by the movies. When Alice was young her mother had prepared for dates while telling the child stories about famous actors and actresses. There were starlets killed by having sex with heavy, important men. 'Torn apart,' Beryl said. These things were hushed up but known to Beryl, who described how men in evening jackets danced out of the wings and knelt at the feet of a haughty beauty who afterwards slept in a bed shaped like a shell. The child listened and drew lines in the spilled face powder on the floor.

There were now empty tables in the Heidelberg and two old men entered and set up a chess board on one of them. Michael lived nearby and gave Alice his address and telephone number which she wrote into her book because, even though he was not a literary person, he was still an intellectual. She walked out into the night with the confident gait of an autodidact, but her buoyant mood vanished when she thought again of Mr Goldman in his hospital bed. Only images of James Chant were powerful enough to distract her.

Alice wanted to know Mr Goldman's first name.

'What's that to you?' Beryl cried, thrusting out her face aggressively. 'All you have to know is, if anybody asks, you're to say he's a friend of the family. What's all this interest in him, anyways?'

'Isn't it normal to know someone's name?' Alice persisted.

'He's nothing to you,' Beryl continued. 'So stay out of it. I seen his will. You get nothing! He's taken care of me and David and if we die first his nephews get everything. He doesn't want his money to go out of his family. Get it? God!' Beryl hooted, wrinkling her face with disgust. 'I can read you like a book.'

The furniture in the room shimmered, drifting off in different directions according to the uneven slope of the floor, and Alice felt herself sliding with them away from Beryl, who crouched like a gargoyle, with darts and invisible lightning flashing out of her in poisonous rays that could penetrate the heart. David stood silently at the front window, his face pressed to the glass where a small circle of condensation haloed the space around his mouth. He breathed noisily as a fine rain quivered to the ground, misting his view of the cars that drove past.

Alice's class had progressed from *Sons and Lovers* to *Women in Love*. There was sex that led to life and sex that led to death; it was like a magical potion that connected some with the infinite and plunged others into nullity.

'There's more to life than sex,' a woman in the class objected.

What a fool, Alice thought. After the class the students clattered out but she lingered beside the window, watching the teacher's reflection in the glass, while he rearranged his papers and books in a worn leather briefcase. After strapping and fastening it he approached and said he wondered if Alice would like to have dinner with him at his place on the weekend. 'Yes,' she agreed gratefully, feeling herself transformed by the alchemy of her teacher's words.

After work Billy picked Alice up in Pete's car, which he'd borrowed for the evening, and they drove to a club. Under a spotlight, a woman in sequins moaned, '*I know how to do it*,' into the microphone and Billy ordered Singapore Slings.

'The *Oriana* came in today,' he told her.

Alice finished all the liquid in her drink and Billy talked about his job; all the accidents that occurred, men knocked unconscious by ropes and thrown into the water. In five years he planned to get his skipper's papers.

The room seemed terribly noisy as Billy snapped his fingers for a waiter. Alice saw a woman wearing a nametag sit down on the banquette next to a small man. The waiter put another drink down in front of Alice and Billy dropped some money on the man's tray. Alice was aware of the nametag woman talking animatedly to the man beside her while he stared straight ahead, his body stiff.

'You're the first friend of Wendy's I've liked, you know,' Billy confided.

At the next table the man got up and walked out without looking back.

'Wendy and I don't really hit it off,' Billy said, squeezing Alice's hand. 'We're too different.' His arm flew up again for the waiter. 'I've been hurt, Alice,' he cried mysteriously. 'I don't tell everyone that.'

Alice stirred her new drink and laid her little swizzle sticks in a row.

'I can't believe I'm telling you these things. Here goes another one: I've never been in love.'

Alice felt sick with fear as Billy made these successive statements. She'd finished the top layer of her drink and could see the pale liquid underneath. Let him not mean me, she prayed, feeling the great void of Billy's potential need sucking at her. When they left he took her arm in the parking lot which was almost empty. To Alice, the car seemed far away and everything looked like it did in a film. She could even see pores in the cool blacktop and dropped to her knees to be closer to its soothing surface.

'Get up, Alice.'

'Leave me alone,' she moaned.

He pulled her to her feet and together they traversed the distance to his car, but the ground seemed to rush up in waves.

'Steady.' Billy guided her into the car.

Why was he pushing her into the back seat? Alice wondered, gazing at stained cloth on the ceiling. The plastic upholstery was warm, clinging to her bare legs and her limbs felt heavy, fleshy and disgusting. Billy's hot body appeared above hers, his knee dug into her, his weight bounced the back seat so she groaned with sickness.

'You're so soft,' he gasped.

His shaved cheek rasped on her skin and she could feel the fibre of his pant leg. 'Leave me alone,' she whispered, forcing the words out between her teeth. She turned her body and pushed at Billy's chest. It surprised her when he tumbled to the floor in slow motion; then her hand rolled down the window and she hung her head over the side to be sick.

'I know you've never been with a man,' Billy said when they pulled up in front of Alice's house. 'That's important to a guy.'

'Like Linda MacIntyre?'

Billy sat up suddenly. 'Who told you that?'

'I just heard it.'

'Heard what?' he asked angrily, pulling a cigarette up from the others in the packet, then raising it to his mouth. He snapped it out of the packet with his lips. 'That story's all lies. Listen, Linda was after me for months. She asked *me*. I never had to promise her nothing. She wanted it.' He drummed his fingers against the steering wheel. 'I can't believe it! She's still telling that same old story.'

Alice studied his face which looked hurt and angry as he breathed heavily and tossed his cigarette out the window. It

· 77 ·

sailed through the air in a shower of sparks. 'Shit!' he said, leaning his head against his arms.

Alice touched his shoulder gingerly. Perhaps it was mean of her to mention Linda MacIntyre. He didn't move so she sat back, wondering if it would be rude to leave him hunched over the wheel like that. Maybe she'd done something very wrong, like in Lawrence's book when Miriam had touched Paul's sides and something in him had flamed up but she'd been unconscious of it. 'Do you want a cigarette?' she asked gently.

He groaned, reaching out to her. 'Just don't mention Linda MacIntyre again.'

'Sorry,' she said, patting his face which lay against her chest, but she was still curious about what Wendy had told her.

'It's okay,' he said in a tired voice, his hand curling around the back of her neck. 'Let's forget it.'

She didn't want to be a sexless priss, the kind Lawrence hated, but there was the other danger, that men would pass her telephone number around and laugh.

'I have to go in.'

'Don't go,' he whispered pathetically, like a child.

She ran up the path leaving him slumped in the front seat of the car. Alcohol. The word with its round syllables sickened her as she stepped quietly into the house.

CHAPTER FIFTEEN

To avoid the possibility of being early for dinner with James, Alice stopped by the library at the corner of Robson and Burrard, only a few blocks from her teacher's place. The library was in a large building with a high ceiling soaring above and a staircase leading up to the fiction section. In winter, old men fell gently asleep at the long reading tables on the main floor.

She stood for a moment gazing towards the stairs, thinking of the way she'd been able to read hundreds, maybe a thousand books, plucking them off shelves and filling her arms the way a hungry person might gather food, hindered only by her inability to carry more at a time, when she felt a hand on her arm. Turning, she saw Michael Halek, the history professor she'd met in the Little Heidelberg Café.

'I saw you come in,' he said, drawing her over to a seat by one of the large windows facing Robson Street. People streamed along the sidewalk outside while they sat talking softly together. Michael's face appeared formidably serious in repose, but when he listened to Alice he smiled gently, saying he liked libraries too, telling her about those in London and Paris where he'd studied. It was in France that he'd been in a bicycle accident that had left his legs paralysed, he said.

'You came home afterwards?' Alice asked, wringing her hands together but keeping her voice matter-of-fact.

'Not right away,' Michael responded. 'I completed my degree first.'

'Yes,' Alice answered nervously.

Michael laughed and took her hand for a minute. 'Cheer up,' he said. 'It happened years ago. You look much too sorrowful.'

When she told him she was walking over to James's for

dinner, Michael accompanied her part of the way, pointing out his house on a quiet street just off Robson. It had an old, weathered porch covered in vines and a large front window where an orange cat peered out.

'I was hoping you'd be one of those rescuing girls,' James exclaimed, pulling the dishtowel from his shoulder when Alice arrived. 'I was working on my thesis and lost track of time,' he added, smiling boyishly and pressing the striped cloth into her hands.

Confused, Alice plucked dishes from the stack in the sink. She'd imagined a beautiful table with candles, but there were teabags and strands of spaghetti in the drain and some of the bowls were filled with bright red mucus.

She was ashamed of her fantasies which she now saw as trite and uneducated. James acted as if the dirty dishes, the absence of food, was completely normal. Intellectuals didn't bother with bourgeois pretentions because their vision of more important, glorious ideas stirred them at all times.

'Sweet and sour sauce,' James explained, leaning against the fridge. She thought his body was just like Paul Morel's or even Lawrence's own. 'Haven't you ever eaten Chinese food?'

Humbly, Alice scraped viscous fluid into the garbage. 'I'll have to introduce you to it,' James went on. The red material slid off the dishes like skin.

'Girls are so generous,' Gordon called out, marching in and stamping through the kitchen, flinging open cupboard doors. 'What happened to that jar of currant jam?'

'Gone.' James lit a cigarette.

'I need a woman to take care of me. To comfort me when I experience the world's rejection,' Gordon said. 'I had a gig and I lost it. I was booked into a restaurant but even that lowly position has been snatched from me.'

Alice swilled dishes through soapy water.

'They hired a bongo player,' Gordon sighed. 'How can I compete?'

Remembering Wendy's talks about the importance of food, Alice was terrified James would find out she was not able to create cunning dishes from the contents of his almost empty cupboards. Her whole future, her entrance into James's world, might depend on him not discovering this fact about her, so she was relieved when the men agreed to pick up Chinese food. After they'd eaten from the white take-out cartons, Gordon begged her not to enter James's room. 'It's more dangerous than Bluebeard's chamber,' he warned, claiming he'd seen other innocent young girls pass through its sinister portals.

Ignoring Gordon's advice, Alice ran her hand along the edge of James's serious desk with its coffee can full of pens and pencils, a stack of white paper and a smaller pile of typed pages. Brooding from the wall above was a large reproduced photograph of D. H. Lawrence. In the corner, a red woollen blanket and a few cushions covered a mattress on the floor. How ordinary and banal her own room seemed by comparison. From the transistor radio beside his bed, Alice could hear an announcer's low, resonant voice describing a sunset over English Bay. 'God!' James exclaimed contemptuously as he turned the dial to an acceptable station. Then he reached out and drew Alice down beside him on the wool blanket while the light notes of a piano floated into the room. I'll never forget this music, she thought when James reached out affectionately to touch her hair, but he recoiled in alarm. 'What makes your hair so stiff?' he demanded.

'Hairspray.'

James poked at her hair tentatively. 'Why don't you just forget about artifice? What would happen?' he asked, fingering the brittle curls that hung in front of her ears. He lit a candle and turned off the light. 'Take out those pins,' he commanded.

Alice knew a whole back-combed thatch would tumble down. 'I can't,' she said, cringing when she heard her voice squeak.

'Let me,' James murmured, but she knew he wouldn't be pleased if he reached his goal so she held her hands up to prevent the release of a hairy cascade.

'You're a shy thing,' he said. 'You need to be properly loved. You've never been properly loved by a man, have you?'

Alice cast her eyes down modestly but she was mortified by his question. Wouldn't it be funny if she said yes? The candle flame shot up and its warm light caught in all the little wires of James's hair and beard when he asked her about her family.

'Really? Your mother virtually lives with someone? That's great!'

'It must be six or seven years.'

James laughed joyfully.

He wanted to know everything about her, especially her childhood which he said was very important.

'My mother sent me in a taxi cab to my aunt's house when I was three,' Alice recalled dreamily. 'I had a little, brown plastic purse with a silver metal clasp. She took down the licence number of the cab so I'd be safe but she didn't come to get me for a couple of years.'

'Poor little lonely thing,' he said, stroking her hand.

'My mother's always going on about some beauty contest she won.'

James drew her head against his chest and she could hear his heart beating. It seemed like a strong heart in such a thin chest but then intellectuals didn't bother to build brutish muscle.

'You've really lived,' he said. 'I was sent to St George's School for Boys.'

Alice moved closer to comfort him.

'Totally divorced from the lived experience of the common man,' James remarked.

'I quit school in grade ten,' Alice said.

'That shows how intelligent and brave you are. I had only intermittent flashes of consciousness until I woke up and found myself in graduate school.' James moved his thumb gently back and forth on her neck.

She wanted to tell him everything about herself.

'You're a pretty little thing,' he said. He wanted to know about Woolworth's and Mr Fordham. James explained that Alice lived a more genuine life than he because his world was artificial and bloodless while her world was root and branch, arterial. His thumb kept rubbing the same place on her neck but she was afraid to move. His thesis was on the man of blood in D. H. Lawrence's novels.

'Are there women of blood?' she inquired.

'Natural women, with their primitive instinctiveness.'

His eyes were half-closed and he leaned on one elbow looking down at her while Alice admired the deep perceptions he had about life.

'There are precious few such women,' James said bitterly, 'especially at university. I don't care for neurotic university women,' he said, holding Alice against him.

'I want to see you naked,' he declared suddenly, pulling at her dress.

She felt ridiculous when she stopped him because she knew that in his sophisticated world people believed in expressing the body's natural impulses.

'You don't trust me yet,' he said. She could have wept at his understanding as she inhaled the fragrance of the Chinese food they'd eaten and felt his beard scrubbing at her cheek. They rested, lying together and smoking cigarettes. He would take her to the art gallery and she would see how glorious nakedness was, not the self-conscious display of flesh but the real thing. There were so many things he wanted to show her, he murmured, breathing smoke into her hair like a dragon.

He was an only child and had been precociously mournful. 'I used to shut myself away in my room and curl up on the window-seat with my books. I was groomed to be an academic. We had guessing games in which someone would play the first few notes of a classical piece. My mother collected art.'

'What does your father do?'

'He's a lawyer.'

Alice wondered if James was making it up.

'What about your father?' James asked her.

'I think he was a cook in the army,' Alice said. Aunt Mavis had declared that he'd been a decent person but Beryl despised him and sometimes puzzled over Alice's paternity, wondering if her father had not actually been some other man. James picked up Alice's hand and enclosed it in his. Her hand looked different held in James's larger one, smaller and paler, as if she were from a different species. Alice told James that when she was young her mother used to take her to roller-skating rinks where she'd watch Beryl whirling with different partners.

'I was always dragged off to the ballet,' James said. 'My parents were obsessed with Europe. There wasn't a bit of life in them.' His eyes were shut and surrounded by shadows like a medieval saint or martyr. 'Europe is a cliché,' he added. 'High school. Then Europe. Then university.' James smiled at her like a child. 'I guess you were free of all that.'

He saw her as natural and not self-conscious she realized, amazed.

'I'm lucky to have met you, aren't I?' he said. 'What if you'd signed up for typing or something, instead of my novel course?'

'You'd have comforted yourself with Mara,' Alice remarked experimentally.

'God! There's nothing genuine about her. That isn't even her real name.'

'But does she do well at university?' Alice asked. 'Is she smart?' Alice hoped she wasn't.

James drew his head back. 'The academic yardstick registers only profound human diminishment,' he said. 'Truly creative intelligences are weeded out ruthlessly. You should see what goes on out there.'

'But don't students gain *something*?'

'Nothing.'

Her eyes were only inches away from his neck and the lively wiry hair of his beard. Her heart really leapt up; she was sure this organ actually bounded forward, just as it was supposed to. There were moments of grace in life in which everything could change in an instant. Music flooded out of the radio in waves like the sea. She'd always hated the sea but now she would glory in all of nature. James pushed her dress off her shoulder and kissed the little peak of bone. When her teacher reached around her back to unclip her brassiere they suddenly heard a woman's voice, singing loudly in the kitchen.

'It's Mara,' James explained as Alice dragged up the front of her dress. 'That damn woman,' he said crossly.

Alone on the bus afterwards, Alice was sustained by a series of images involving James possibly descending upon her in a dark rush, the annihilation of the paltry thing she was and her potential transformation.

The lights were blazing when she reached her house and Billy staggered back and forth across the front lawn, shouting he was going to kill her. Tightly wrapped in a bathrobe, Beryl stood outlined in the window as Billy's thick figure roamed the yard, stumbling over the piece of wood David had leaned against one of the scrubby cedar trees. Alice crept to the lane and came quietly through the back door.

'It's not my fault,' she hissed when she saw Beryl's face.

'You must have led him on.'

'I didn't.'

'The girl's the one with the will-power.'

'I'll kill you!' Billy howled.

Beryl stepped backwards. 'The stupid jerk. That's what you get when you mix with the scum.'

Billy stared into the night, his arms hanging loosely at his sides when Alice ventured on to the front porch. His head turned slowly towards her and she saw his dark suit torn at the shoulder. 'You been out with that guy who got you to read dirty books,' he wept, staggering towards the gate. 'Your mother told me all about it. I had a fight tonight because of you. My hundred dollar suit is ripped,' he sobbed.

'Clear out,' Beryl snarled, hairpins bristling from the row of pincurls around her face.

'My girlfriend's a whore!' Billy cried. Then he slammed the door of the car and roared off with tyres screaming.

'This place isn't going to turn into a brothel no matter what you think. Mr Goldman's going to be DISGUSTED when I tell him what you've been up to. You think you can fool people but I can see right through you!' Beryl shouted.

Alice breathed shallowly and didn't answer.

On the bus in the morning, Alice stared up at the happy, smooth faces in the advertisements overhead as she reviewed her evening with James, wondering if she'd been too forward or too reserved. Poetesses, interpretive dancers might pass through James's flat in an unending flow, whispering poetry. During her break, she called Wendy from the pay phone while she gazed at the floor of the booth strewn with gum wrappers and cigarette butts. Her feet looked swollen, her ankles thick and unlovable.

'Was it your first date?' Wendy asked.

'He wants everything to be natural and open,' Alice explained.

'Of course he'd say that.'

'I can't bear it if he doesn't phone,' Alice moaned. 'He's the only person I know who likes D. H. Lawrence.'

'You're weird sometimes, Alice,' Wendy sighed.

On her lunch break Alice called James even though she was sick with fear, imagining his possible coolness or even contempt at being phoned by a shopgirl. How peculiar he might think her as she stood there in her puffy Woolworth's smock, but her hand reached out for the phone as if controlled by some hypnotic command.

'I'm so glad you phoned,' he said in a low voice full of warmth and intimacy, and she was weak with relief seeing the sun glancing off cars moving busily along Hastings Street. The sounds of the city suggested progress and hope, the practical pragmatism of men pulling down old structures and erecting new ones while workers hung suspended above the street. James wanted to meet her family and she called her mother to warn her that she'd be bringing him home. 'Is that okay?' she asked, but Beryl wouldn't answer because she was still angry.

James was lounging against a lamppost and smoking a cigarette when Alice ran out of the store at closing time. He was wearing a shirt of some soft material open at the collar and his bare feet were thrust into moccasins. Even the thoughtful way he exhaled a thin stream of cigarette smoke was intense and carelessly elegant. His eyes were approving when they reached Alice's house and he saw high grass in the yard where an old lawnmower stood locked with rust. Alice pushed open the door, not knowing what she'd find.

'It's me,' she called out like Mr Goldman did, wondering now if his habitual announcement had implied a warning.

Beryl sat demurely on the couch with her legs crossed and her wide feet encased in black, toeless sandals. Alice had never seen the dress her mother was wearing, a grey wool sheath, too warm for summer. Her mother's face appeared smaller than usual and her suspicious, childlike eyes were wide, as if fixed on some terrible vision. On the floor, David was unscrewing the back of another old radio.

'It's about time we met,' Beryl leered up at James. Her hair was brushed wetly and her lips were incarnadine. 'So you're the one who's been keeping my daughter out half the night.'

'I'm afraid so,' James agreed pleasantly.

'You didn't tell me he's got a beard,' Beryl complained to Alice. 'I've always liked men with beards. Anyways, what's this out-all-night stuff?'

'I suppose we lost track of time,' James remarked. 'I was telling Alice there are sleep debts and we can catch up on weekends.'

'Oh yeah?' Beryl sneered, puffing vigorously on her cigarette. 'Who says?' She wagged her foot back and forth and Alice saw her mother's toenails were ridged and filthy. Beryl insisted dirt was healthy. She bathed infrequently but with much ceremony, sitting in greyish water in the tub while wearing a brassiere and keeping a washcloth arranged between her legs like a loincloth.

'Scientists. Or so I've read,' James told her.

'Huh!' Beryl said, blowing out a gust of smoke. 'Alice tells me you're some kind of professor or something.'

'What?' James asked while Alice cringed in her chair.

'That's enough of that! "Pardon" will do,' Beryl cried raucously, throwing her head back in a peal of laughter at her joke. Then she bounded up as if struck by revelation. 'Stay right there,' she commanded, motioning to James. When she left the room Alice glanced at James but he only sat back comfortably on the couch while David stared at him. The window was a black, uncurtained square that reflected the room and Alice was dismayed to see her own face looking young and not at all sophisticated.

'Ta-da!' Beryl sang nasally from the hallway, and she minced into the room with one hand on her hip, wearing only a black bathing suit and high-heeled sandals; the suit made of thick elastic material that cut into the tops of her thighs. Her calves were covered with coarse dark hair, but she was proud of this hirsuteness and had boasted to Alice that men considered this feature sexy. Alice thought this was unbelievable and disgusting. The bathing suit Beryl wore was strapless and its boned top protruded in two pointed peaks where the bodice was incompletely filled with flesh. There was a panel across the belly which did not hide the plump triangle of cloth between Beryl's legs as she pirouetted in front of James.

'Not bad, eh?' she cried in triumph.

'Mom,' David begged.

James shouted with laughter and Alice sat stiffly in Mr Goldman's chair, gripping the arms.

Gaily, her lipsticked mouth open in a wide showgirl's smile, Beryl wriggled from the room, kicking out her leg and waving her hand at the doorway.

James claimed to have enjoyed the meeting immensely.

'Freud would have a field day at your house,' he whispered on the front porch when he was leaving.

CHAPTER SIXTEEN

ALICE THOUGHT IT unlikely that James knew how to fight and she hoped he wouldn't have to. Yet as they left Woolworth's on Friday night and strolled along the sidewalk through warm summer air a car kept pace with them, swerved to a stop and a man leapt out, staggering threateningly and brandishing a beer bottle. Alice had been preoccupied by James's energetic conversation and the fact that he knew everything about the movie they intended to see, including the names of the director and producer. When she saw Billy lurching in the street, grasping a bottle like a weapon, her body became electric with fear while her mind underwent an immediate paralysis of boredom. Life was so unfair – even one's own suffering was uninteresting.

'Do you know this guy?' James asked, looking from Billy to Alice.

She nodded resentfully, shocked that a man from the past could veer into a totally different present and change everything.

Billy growled threateningly and swayed back and forth. Alice remembered hearing something about Billy and a court case resulting from a fight in a beer parlour.

'She's my woman,' Billy declared thickly, smashing the bottle on to his borrowed car so broken glass gushed over the hood in a shower of glittering shards. He gripped the jagged neck of the bottle in his large hand, his narrowed eyes aggrieved and excited.

'I think Alice can choose her man,' James remarked.

James thought this was a discussion, Alice realized with dismay.

Billy breathed noisily and gazed at James with hatred.

'Get your car out of the way,' they heard a woman yell from the large automobile behind Pete's car which Billy had abandoned in the street, blocking the lane.

With a howl, Billy lunged into the road and tore open the driver's door while the woman's husband jumped sideways into his wife's lap, holding his hands up protectively. Alice guided James into an alley and led him swiftly past grey buildings towards a street in Chinatown. She imagined Billy tearing along behind them with his jagged bottle, but James kept telling her not to hurry. 'I'll protect you,' he said consolingly.

They hurled themselves into the front seat of a bus heading for the University of British Columbia and James explained Alice's fear was natural under the circumstances. 'The hens cower while the cocks fight,' he said, taking her hand and clasping it in his own while the bus strained up Tenth Avenue hill.

James led her to the cashier's window of the Varsity Theatre, past the man in a wine-coloured jacket who took their tickets. The movie was about a man Alice hated, but James sat forward alertly, stroking his beard from time to time and when it was over, he remained in his seat, his gaze riveted on the credits.

'Consider Joe Lampdon's dilemma,' James said of the main character when they made their way out. 'He was forced to choose between an unacceptable relationship with a woman he loved and an appropriate marriage with a woman he didn't. If he stayed with the Simone Signoret character, he'd hate her finally, because his ambitions would be unfulfilled. And what gave him such ambitions? Modern industrial society.'

Alice pushed open the door of the Varsity Grill, the sudden brightness startling after the dark theatre. There were two rows of wooden booths and a line of stools at the shining counter under vivid depictions of milkshakes, sundaes and hamburgers.

'Society has to have an alienated male population to keep industry moving,' James said as they sat in a small booth and a waiter handed them menus. The other waiters stood in a huddle at the back of the restaurant chatting in Cantonese. According to James, this café sold monthly meal tickets to students and the waiters knew all their regular customers by name. 'Society hates and destroys anything that interferes with making money, like sex and beauty,' James cried. 'Especially sex because it makes people beautiful. Beauty doesn't result from a certain shape of nose or face, it's generated by sex-glow. That's what makes Simone Signoret attractive.'

'Wasn't Signoret actually beautiful?'

'No,' James said. 'Without the fire of sex rising in her Simone Signoret would be a putty-faced, middle-aged woman.'

They ordered tea and french fries while a group of people came in, talking and laughing, and took the booth next to the restaurant's front window.

'Some women sell their sacred fire,' James said when the waiter set down little metal teapots on thick saucers. 'Not you though. You're natural and instinctive, unspoiled.' They shared hot pieces of potato from a plate in the middle of the table, while James explained roosters were always lively with colour and concentration. Billy had done the right thing by crowing and rustling his feathers at a rival male and Alice's henny role was to stand aside.

'That sounds so ignoble,' Alice objected.

James made a sound of contempt. 'Nobility,' he exclaimed. 'That's just an idea. Instinct and passion are important.'

What she couldn't grasp, the next day at work when Mr Fordham held her own order form in front of her, was how people who never bothered to read D. H. Lawrence could never-theless unerringly perform tasks that were beyond her. Each time she made a stock order she suffered when she observed the mysterious columns and boxes on her form, but her co-workers seemed to make swift accurate calculations. According to Mr Fordham, she was guilty of ordering a gross of raffia belts when dozens of that same item remained on the stockroom shelves. The F. W. Woolworth's chain was built on the concept of fast stock turnover. As Mr Fordham outlined the problem Alice felt her thinking grow slower and duller until her face assumed a gape of stupidity. Paul Morel's quick mind could adapt to anything, darting quickly and competently from bookkeeping to art, languages and algebra. What if she, Alice, were a kind of oddity, like mentally handicapped children who could play one piece of brilliant music on the violin or something? As Beryl said, no one would give a job to a person whose only skill was reading novels. What if it turned out that the only thing she rapturously cared for was utterly useless?

CHAPTER SEVENTEEN

BERYL DECIDED James was leading Alice towards destruction. 'He's hot to trot,' she said broodingly, her eyes on the television screen. The pictures helped her concentration and she uttered conclusions about life during commercials. Maggie had advised Beryl to use psychology. The best way to stop Alice from going out with James was to be overwhelmingly hospitable to him and his family. 'I'm going to make him sick of the sight of you,' Beryl crowed. 'You sick of the sight of him, I mean,' she corrected herself. 'Wait and see.' After hunting for the telephone book, she called his mother and invited the family for dinner.

'It's going to be horrible,' Alice wailed. She and James sat in his kitchen eating toast and marmalade.

'My mother feels she should have some idea of your background,' James explained. 'It won't be as bad as you think. My parents need to get out of their circle of neutered Kerrisdalites.'

'What's he going on about?' Gordon marched in and straddled a chair. James had told Alice that Gordon's girlfriend was frigid because she willed herself not to submit.

'James's parents are going to meet my mother.'

Gordon reached out and plucked a piece of toast from her plate. 'That's normal,' he said cheerfully, biting into the bread. He was in a good mood because he'd been promised a gig at a club that featured folk singers.

Alice had a vision of her mother sitting on the edge of the couch, holding a teacup in one hand, perhaps dropping ash into the saucer; her mother crossing her thickly-haired legs while James's mother, dressed neatly in beige, pretended such legs were normal.

'Don't pay any attention to him,' James commented. 'He goes to mass.' Gordon was doomed by his predilection for vamps, James said. This demonstrated his fear of true womanliness and sex.

Alice's mind was preoccupied with the coming dinner. She recalled nervously that when her mother used the toilet, she left the door wide open and anyone could hear her bladder emptying, like a horse in a barn.

Mr Goldman had left the hospital to stay with his family in Florida where he'd lounge in a garden bright with sun. Beryl smoothed out his postcards and stared at the pictures suspiciously. 'I could buy him an orange at Safeway if that's what he wants,' she said. 'I don't trust that family of his.' However, she was fired with her new project. 'Sunday dinner,' she'd told James's mother, 'with the family.'

Beryl planned the menu with Maggie: roast beef, mashed potatoes, gravy and frozen peas would be laid out in cut glass dishes Maggie would lend Beryl for the occasion. Maggie was a doll, Beryl cried. For dessert, according to Maggie, something simple and light was in order, like fruit salad. Beryl was going to buy the brand containing greater numbers of maraschino cherries than inferior kinds. Maggie lent dessert cups with flowers etched on the sides. 'Don't put too much food in your mouth at once,' Beryl warned David who was accustomed to eating out of a bowl in front of the television. A list was made in Beryl's erratic handwriting, outlining preparations. Alice's job was to wash walls and David was to put away the boxes of metal bits he'd taken out of the old radios.

Alice started at the tops of the walls and scrubbed. 'The walls were green before,' she called out as the paint melted away. The water was black with filth.

Beryl tied her hair in a scarf and rolled up her sleeves. She removed the contents of a kitchen cupboard, and found a child's tooth in an eggcup, the stub of an old candle and a mouldy photograph of a friend she didn't speak to any more. 'What do I need three salt cellars for?' she laughed, amazed. The counter was covered with unmatched dishes, a toothpick holder, dusty plastic bowls, washers and bits of string. To revive herself,

Beryl made another pot of tea and sat down with her feet up because she didn't want to get veins.

She watched critically while Alice began another wall. 'You're getting streaks,' she observed, holding up her pearly orange mug of tea. 'Change the water.'

Alice, balancing on the shaky kitchen chair, peered into the murky plastic pail.

'Lookit this woman on TV,' Beryl cried. 'Winning a mink coat and a trip to Hawaii. The old bag. Lookit. Why don't I ever win nothing?' Later she shoved all the things on the kitchen counter into drawers and cupboards. 'It's a bit better, anyways,' she said, wiping her hands on the back of her shorts. 'I can't do everything, you know. I'm only human.'

When the day came, Alice arose early and found Beryl sitting at the kitchen table, writing on a torn bit of paper. 'I'm making a plan,' she said, her face haggard.

James arrived first, striding confidently up the path, avoiding the wet touch of the long grass.

'Wine! We'll have a hot time in the old town tonight, eh?' Beryl laughed tensely, taking the bottle from him. She wore a black crêpe dress and she'd tied a tea towel around her waist. Preoccupied, she glanced at her list and ran her hands over the table she and Alice had dragged into the back of the living room. They'd agreed James's parents could not see the kitchen.

Beryl had produced a lace tablecloth from her old trunk but it was too large for the table, so they folded the pale lace in a ridge across the centre.

'Is that a stain?'

'It's only water. I'll put a plate on it.'

Alice and Beryl had collected all the bits and pieces and put them in a box in the basement. When they'd staggered down the stairs with the carton, they'd been astounded by the number of things already stored in the dark cellar, covered with dust and webs.

At Maggie's, Beryl bought a little runner edged with careful embroidery and laid this on top of the television where she set a glass candy dish filled with mints David had been warned not to eat.

James settled himself on the couch, stretching the bedspread that covered this piece of furniture so the ripped upholstery underneath was revealed. Then he held out a book. '*Lady Chatterley's Lover*,' he murmured, presenting it to Alice. 'I've never given a woman a book before.'

Alice displayed the volume on the television beside the mints, thinking the gift of a novel by Lawrence was more profound than anything else James might have given her. It seemed a kind of pledge. When she looked out the window to see James's parents coming up the walk, she didn't care about the dead bluebottles lying on the sill.

The doorbell made a faint sound.

'Do I look okay?' There was sweat on Beryl's forehead and upper lip.

'Answer it!' Alice cried. Her mother's skin appeared sallow against the black dress and her lips were as red as a vampire's.

'Come in, come in,' Beryl yelled, laughing a dry 'ack, ack' of sound and throwing open the door. 'We're ready for you!'

A small woman in a beige dress walked in followed by a heavily built man in a grey suit. James's mother had soft, neatly waved brown hair and a string of pearls at her throat. His father's thick reddish hair was turning grey and he thrust his neck forward as he entered.

'So this is Alice,' he boomed.

Alice was struck dumb with shyness.

'Sit down,' Beryl cried. 'I'll have everything ready in a minute.' A strand of hair was stuck to her lip.

The men stood and waited while Mrs Chant lowered herself gracefully into Mr Goldman's chair and Beryl scuttled back to the kitchen.

'James tells me you work at Woolworth's,' Mrs Chant began.

Nodding, Alice glanced desperately at the kitchen door.

'I've been quite busy myself, haven't I, dear?' James's mother asked, looking at her husband, who didn't answer. 'It's the golf tournament soon.' She turned to Alice. 'I garden too.'

Alice thought Mr Chant was looking up her skirt so she tugged at her hem.

'Mother! You have a gardener,' James interjected.

'I know, dear, but if the gardener doesn't do something, I have to do it. It's not as simple as you think.'

Mr Chant pushed himself out of the chair and took a mint from the dish, cracking it loudly between his teeth. 'James tells me your father died when you were a baby.'

'He *may* be dead. We don't know for sure,' Alice qualified.

Dinner began badly when David came to the table with his hands filthy and had to be sent back to wash them again. His tears fell on the bits of chopped lettuce and tomato on his plate.

'Sensitive,' Beryl explained, winking. 'He'll grow out of it.'

James told his father divorce was better for the children than an unhappy marriage.

'I was just a kid when I married the first time,' Beryl confided, splashing wine into her glass.

Alice and David both looked up.

'However, my second marriage is perfectly happy,' she claimed.

Certain everyone could hear disgusting sounds, Alice wondered if James's parents thought they ate like animals. Beryl cleared away the salad plates and brought in a platter with a dark roast on it.

'It's bleeding!' David warned.

'It's supposed to,' Beryl replied, placing a bowl of potatoes and a gravy boat beside it. She'd instructed them to act as if this was their regular family dinner. 'Will you carve?' she asked, smiling at Mr Chant who jumped up and ferociously wielded the carving knife she handed him.

Then they all had to hang on to the table to steady it as he drew the knife across the meat. It was very hot in the room and Beryl fanned her face with one of the paper napkins she'd bought. Alice gripped the edge of the table wondering if she should have electrolysis done on the hair of her arms.

'Just pot luck, I'm afraid!' Beryl cried, her eyes on Mr Chant's flushed face.

'I'll bet you're a great help to your mother,' Mrs Chant said to David.

Mouth bulging with food, David stared at her silently.

'He's shy,' Beryl explained quickly. 'Gets it from me. I didn't open my mouth when I was a kid.' She grimaced and laughed. 'I guess those times are gone forever.'

'I suppose property values might very well go up around here someday,' Mr Chant said, gazing about.

'For God's sake, Father.' James put down his fork.

Mr Chant bent his head towards Beryl, who was tilting back her glass. There were little bits of dried mascara around her eyes.

'Kids!' Beryl laughed falsely. 'They put on airs at that age.'

Alice stared at the mound of meat on her plate.

'Have you been playing much tennis lately, Dad?' James asked.

Mr Chant, digging into his dish while tilting it away from him, said he'd had no time.

'I played tennis at the Y when I was young,' Beryl reminisced. 'I was good too but no one encouraged me.' She looked woefully at the tablecloth that had been pulled awry.

'What a shame,' Mrs Chant exclaimed.

'I was a wonderful skater, too. You shoulda seen me do figure eights.' Beryl took a piece of gristle from her mouth and laid it delicately on the side of her plate.

James's hands were so much more alive than those of other people, Alice thought. She could hear her mother talking boringly on about her athletic abilities while Mr Chant's neck, flushed with the heat of the food and wine, folded walrus-like on to his collar. How could he have fathered someone as thin and graceful as James? She studied James's hands, knowing he would save her from the horror of the mundane.

'God helps those who help themselves!' Beryl shouted. 'Do you need any secretaries in that big office of yours? Like my daughter here? She's willing to learn, as they say.' Beryl rolled her eyes.

'Mother! I don't even know how to type!' Alice cried, flushing with mortification.

'Why don't you send in a résumé?' Mrs Chant suggested.

'I've already got a job,' Alice said, her voice high and anxious.

'So? You want to work in a Five and Dime all your life?' Beryl rubbed her thumb and fingers together. 'Think big. If you don't want the money you could always give it to me. Ha, ha.'

Mr and Mrs Chant left the maraschino cherries uneaten.

'Some men pursue ambition like machines,' James said, 'but women can't bear that kind of emptiness.'

'Men make sacrifices to provide for their families, James.' Mr Chant folded his big hands together on the tablecloth.

'Their families don't want a machine; they want a man.'

Alice liked to hear James pronounce the word 'man'.

'Some men are real bastards though,' Beryl mused, waving her glass. 'When I was pregnant, her father made me sleep on the floor.'

Mrs Chant stared. 'Why?'

'He was a pervert.'

'Do you think he was?' Alice asked James after his parents had walked gratefully out the gate. Alice's head was on James's chest and she imagined a passer-by might think they'd been together for years. The rain had stopped suddenly and the front yard was a sodden tangle; the air smelled of decay and worms moved delicately and blindly across broken cement. Mrs Chant had screamed as she'd picked her way through, clinging to her husband's arm.

'Jeez, what's this? Young love?' Beryl screeched behind them.

'Don't worry,' James said. 'Perversion results from boredom.'

CHAPTER EIGHTEEN

SOUND CASCADED over Alice when James and Gordon led her into the brightly-lit parlour at the Cecil Hotel, explaining everything to her while she listened hungrily and gazed at the sights. Serious drinkers downed beer at tables glistening with liquid, but she looked away from these people to avoid drifting into tranced, stupefying misery, concentrating instead on those pointed out by her companions – students, poets, the leader of the Communist Party of Canada (Marxist Leninist), and a knot of young men in red, engineering students' jackets.

'I'm too nice,' Gordon told Alice, swinging his head around to search for unattached women. He expelled a mournful breath. 'Women prefer assassins.'

'Niceness is pure egotism,' James commented.

The doors of the beer parlour swung open and closed again as people passed in and out; then Alice glimpsed Michael Halek. He paused just inside the entrance and Alice jumped up and waved. By the time he'd reached them, she'd already imagined a long, intense friendship among the three men and herself. While they shook hands she could see them in the future lounging about in a large studio in Paris, comparing ideas beneath skylights admitting beautiful, revivifying light. No, she revised, there would be poetry and a smell of paint. Their work would be galvanizing and passionate and they would go to cafés in the evenings where they would drink liquids out of tiny, exquisite glasses. She and James would cast secret glances at each other which would not be missed by their friends. Now James began to speak about the man of blood and how the body was not capable of dishonesty. Alice studied the strings of bubbles in her glass, while Michael rested his elbows on the arms of his chair and clasped his large hands together, steepling his thumbs while he listened. Alice noticed the tendons fanning across the backs of his hands which were well-shaped and strong.

'Modern man has abandoned his connection with his solar plexus!' James complained.

Michael's face was attentive, but he gave the impression that James's speech occupied only a small portion of his consciousness. 'You're a victim of a metaphor,' Michael told James, his voice preoccupied.

'Oh, God,' Gordon groaned, signalling to the waiter for more beer.

'You're simply transferring beliefs about the mind and the soul to the body,' Michael pointed out calmly.

'*We are, we are, we are the engineers,*' the engineers began to sing, raising their glasses to toast themselves.

A superior smile pulled at James's lips and his colour rose. He caught Alice's gaze and she knew she was supposed to signal her alliance with him and his statements. Michael was watching her too. Her stomach contracted but she made herself gaze back at James with innocent blankness.

Gordon gestured towards the engineering students who had jumped up and were now marching through the beer parlour, snaking between the tables. 'These people,' he said, 'are untouched by even the faintest suggestion of an idea or thought.'

James corrected him at once. 'They have ideas but they're shoddy and superficial,' he said, yanking back his chair and turning towards the men in red windbreakers, who seized a weedy fellow in a tweed jacket and hoisted him on to their shoulders.

Alice couldn't understand how the situation could be veering off so wrongly from the ideal one she'd imagined. She could scarcely believe the scarlet-jacketed men were university students. She wondered if there was a remark she might make that would change the nature of the evening, some fascinating observation that would unite James and Michael, so that their initial sparring would be the intellectual counterpart of a Laurentian wrestling match.

'Doesn't this make you question the fundamental beliefs of democracy?' James inquired, indicating the engineers. 'Equality! What a banal sentiment that is.'

Michael's gaze was sardonic when it rested upon Alice. She was certain James didn't really mean what he said, but she feared Michael wouldn't understand that such statements burst out of James despite the originality of his mind. His sensitivity caused him to be irritable and to say things he didn't really believe.

Waiters were unable to penetrate the jostling red circle of engineers who set their victim on a table where he stood helplessly, a pale young man with thin, untidy hair and a shamed smile.

He wasn't only opposed to democracy but socialism as well, James said, any political philosophy that robbed the individual of his identity as a divine creature.

As if a single entity, the engineers turned, swerved between the tables and stamped out, roaring, 'We are! We are!', their eyes glittering with violent rapture.

James continued to catalogue the political movements with which he did not agree. 'I'm against anything that stifles the blood beat of life,' he cried. Saying this, his voice grew higher and he threw his arm around Alice's shoulders, looking around in triumph.

Michael's face became perfectly still as James's voice went on, and then Alice grew conscious of someone standing beside her. When she turned her head she saw a smooth expanse of hairless abdomen; a man wavered beside the table, his shirt partly unbuttoned and pulled out of his waistband. Alice could smell the drunk's skin and observe its fine texture. Let this not be happening, she prayed. James was telling Michael that life had unity and grand design but this could only be created by the instincts of the body. Was she the only one who could see the man standing next to her? Alice wondered.

'Want to buy a shirt?' the man moaned beside Alice. It was like some kind of a play in which everyone had the wrong script, Alice thought. The man had confused, grieving eyes and a red mouth. Alice saw Michael's attention turn from James to the man who was now dragging at his buttons.

'Come on,' the man wheedled. 'Two bucks. Just two lousy bucks. Have a heart,' he begged, his thick fingers fumbling with the plastic discs. 'It's a good shirt.'

Deprived of his audience James ceased his exposition and swivelled his head towards the man. After a moment, he leapt up, eyes flashing. 'I'll buy it, my good man,' he cried, unfolding a two-dollar bill from his pocket.

The man reached towards the money but James held it away. 'No, not until I have the shirt,' he said almost lovingly, keeping his eyes fixed on the man.

With slow movements, the man unfastened the garment and cloth drifted from his shoulders which were plump and smooth, the skin very fine and milky. His belly indented softly at the umbilicus. When he caught his arm in one of the sleeves he looked around pleadingly for help.

'Give him the money,' Alice cried, looking away. She heard cloth tear and then felt the man's shirt fall softly on to her head like a mantle, covering her face in a warm, smothering flash of white. Michael reached out to help when she yanked the material away.

'I would have robbed him of his dignity if I hadn't taken that shirt,' James informed the others as the man stumbled off. 'I would have been treating him like a beggar,' he went on, his face exalted.

'He *was* a beggar,' Alice insisted, watching the man fall into an empty chair.

'I respected his integrity,' James said.

'You showed him he still had something left to sell,' Michael responded.

With a sigh of exasperation, James changed the subject. There surely was a kind of design in life, he said. It flamed up naturally. But Michael replied that James had been led astray, seduced by his own need rather than evidence, selecting interpretations of experience that suited his interests.

'How else would one select?' James inquired. He didn't notice the shirtless man being led out into the street.

Alice herself tried not to remember this man the next day when she set a jar of blossoms on the table beside Mr Goldman's chair. Everyone in the house was awaiting Mr Goldman's arrival from Florida. He was taking a taxi directly from the airport.

'Goldie doesn't go for flowers and all that palaver,' Beryl objected as she paced back and forth, her eyes flashing, ashes falling from her cigarette. She said she didn't know why she let herself get all upset over Goldie when he didn't give a thought to her.

'When's he coming?' David asked.

'His plane's already in,' Beryl snapped. 'You can't just walk off a plane, you know. It's not like a bus.'

Alice laughed.

'What's so funny?' Beryl puffed furiously at her cigarette. 'Once I went to New York and they looked through all my stuff, even my underwear. I was going to see your father. What a mistake that was. He was on leave.'

'Whose father?'

'Hers,' Beryl yelled. 'Yours'll be here soon. Just look out the window and shut up and don't bug me.'

'Didn't you ever love him?' Alice asked.

'What?' Beryl looked up. 'Don't get me started on that subject. Boy, I could tell you some stories about him. I didn't have a life of ease, like you. Even though I won a beauty contest when I was fourteen, nobody ever gave me nothing.'

'I've thought of looking him up,' Alice said.

'Oh yeah? You and the FBI.'

'What do you mean?'

Beryl's lips thinned. 'He had something wrong with him, that's for sure. Was he ever twisted.'

David bobbed up and down when the yellow taxi stopped at the front gate but Beryl sauntered to the door and flung it open, leaning against the doorjamb casually, one hip thrust out. 'Get ready. Go get his bags, David.' The taxi driver walked slowly around the car and opened the trunk. The back door of the cab stood ajar. 'What is this? *Suspense Theatre*?' Beryl called out, wagging her hips. Mr Goldman stepped carefully on to the sidewalk. 'Jeez, look at that. He's black!' Beryl cried. David darted down the walk and Mr Goldman put his hand on the child's shoulder as they came up the path together. The taxi driver sprang up the porch with a suitcase in each hand. 'He'll pay,' Beryl said with a laugh. 'I just live here.'

Mr Goldman walked slowly to his chair. He wore a light grey suit and matching fedora and his thin face was brown from the Florida sun. He set his hand gingerly on the table where the buttercups wobbled as David scrambled into his lap.

'Get rid of that junk,' Beryl ordered, pointing at the flowers. 'Make tea. Don't climb on him, David.'

Alice threw the flowers into the trash under the sink and when she opened the cupboard, a warmish scent of decay seeped out. From the other room she heard Mr Goldman answering Beryl's questions, remarking that his time in Florida had been pleasant and Alice stopped to consider this mild, spacious word.

'I suppose they keep everything separate from everything else,' Beryl complained. 'God, you'd always be in the kitchen; life's too short for that.'

They sat together in the living room watching a show on television in which a dog befriended a raccoon and stuck loyally by it, even when other canines formed a snarling circle underneath the tree where the terrified animal hid. Even species loyalty was weaker than love. Mr Goldman had to wipe his eyes. When Alice got up in the morning he'd already left, taking his suitcases to his brother-in-law's.

Alice imagined Mr Goldman's other home to be sunny and clean, filled with books and comfortable furniture that matched. The nephews she'd heard about planned to be doctors or lawyers. They craved hamsters, gerbils and exotic birds but soon tired of these pets which were given away and replaced by others. Alice had once caught a glimpse of one of these indulged and clever children, a serious boy with red hair who'd sat beside Mr Goldman in a large car that had pulled up in front of the house.

Beryl said Mr Goldman must never know about Alice's terrible carryings-on during his absence. The first time he'd ever seen Alice he'd told Beryl she was a perfect young lady but now he was disappointed, Beryl claimed, telling Alice sex was like mashed potatoes and Alice was a fool to think otherwise. Who would risk ruin for mashed potatoes?

Alice wondered if a soul was a useless thing, given to ecstasies in the presence of literature but doomed to immoderate suffering when faced with ordinary life. When she gazed at Mr Goldman's grave profile, she felt as if her soul flew out towards him, hovering invisibly in useless cherishing motions like an impotent angel.

She was reading *Lady Chatterley's Lover*. James said Constance Chatterley had been drifting towards death before she met the gamekeeper. There was nothing more despicable than a timid, soulful virgin, he added, but Alice thought it was terrible that Mellors told all those things about his wife so Lady Chatterley could feel such smirking, easy superiority.

James began to meet Alice after work, watching as she covered the counters with dustsheets, and waiting outside after closing time when clerks filed past Chuck who stood guard at the door to check packages and bags. Afterwards, Alice and James walked clasped together along the beach and gazed at the mountains growing distant and blue, overlapping each other delicately, like shapes cut out of tissue paper. In the hushed darkness after sunset they spoke softly to each other, hypnotized by the languid tones of their own voices and the rhythmic sound of waves moving like breath. Night opened around them suggesting infinite space and possibility. It was the ordinariness of love that amazed Alice, James's hand warm against her waist, its shape and pressure concentrated with meaning, endowed with the stunning idea that lives could be linked. When they were cold they rushed into the heat of a fish and chip shop near the beach or ate bortsch at the Little Heidelberg Café. Although they found themselves gripped by sudden hunger their needs were fretfully precise and specific. Only certain foods could satisfy the exact quality of their desires.

Beryl complained Alice was rarely home and it was true she usually caught the last bus and awakened exhausted in the morning. Her chores remained unperformed and Beryl tossed the pile of unwashed laundry down the basement stairs. At work only the force of Alice's will defied her desire for sleep;

yet when James appeared she was electric, filled with energy.

Mr Fordham said he wanted to talk to her and Alice feared he'd noticed her weariness. She could smell his perfumed aftershave lotion as he stood beside her, rocking back and forth and clasping his hands behind his back. Her mother had been in to see him, he said. 'She wants me to fire you,' Mr Fordham went on, 'because she says your reputation will hurt the business of the store.'

Alice could scarcely hear him at all, just a faint drone. She imagined her mother's excited, nasal voice panting and gasping in Mr Fordham's clean, snail-shaped ears, supplying stories about Alice and outlining her own maternal tribulations.

'Your reputation is none of my business,' Mr Fordham said.

Alice knew it was useless to begin to explain because of the complicated details that would have to be supplied and the unbelievable nature of the evidence. Besides, how boring. The thin wooden floorboards seemed hypnotically interesting and she studied every detail of their whorls and patterns.

'As long as you perform your work in the store I'm not concerned with what you do outside,' said Mr Fordham.

Alice nodded dumbly.

'Why do you let it get to you?' James exclaimed later. 'Who are these people? What do you care what they think of you?' He took her to a poetry reading and she was surprised to see the poet was not at all slender and romantic, but was instead a squat, powerful man with bad skin who shouted poems while pacing wildly across the tiny stage in the dim coffee house. The man was dressed carelessly in ugly clothes like a derelict and it was said he carried sheets of his poetry in shopping bags.

At Woolworth's, a cashier was absent and Alice took over one of the cash registers at the front of the store. The work was simple and repetitive, allowing her to descend into a dreamy trance while her hand lifted and fell on the keys, ripping off the tape when the machine completed its interior convulsions. The cashier had to be vigilant, however, because Woolworth's employed 'shoppers', ordinary-looking women who arrived at the register with packets of nylon stockings slipped inside record jackets and price tickets from lower-priced merchandise pinned to costly items. When Alice went on her break Diane took over. Mr Fordham was training her in all aspects of the business and had already promised her the coveted job of whipping hot wax into froth to cover the Christmas candles. The clerk who did this would spend a week in the stockroom with tables full of candles sprinkled with glitter. Mr Fordham considered Diane artistic.

'When we tallied the cash last night it was short,' Mr Fordham told Alice the next day while she stood in the office where she'd been summoned. 'You were the last person on the till,' he added. Alice pictured bills stuck together, perhaps carelessly passed to a dishonest customer or her fingers slipping to the wrong keys.

'We can't prove who it was,' said Mr Fordham.

'If you think I took the money, I'd like to quit,' Alice choked out.

Mr Fordham looked up at her. 'We'll give you your vacation pay in lieu of notice.'

'Why don't you work at the university?' James asked, holding a piece of toast on the palm of his hand while he spread blackcurrant jam on it. His hair was still damp and toast crumbs fell on to his beard as he ate.

'But I haven't finished high school,' Alice wailed. She'd hurtled out of Woolworth's before her shift had finished, catching the Robson Street bus in the middle of the day like someone on holiday. James's advice was freeing and interesting with its suggestion that there had been something unnecessarily humble and ridiculous about the way she'd filled in application forms in the past, neatly printing the true answers in the relevant spaces. What he really meant was that truth was a flowing revelation, not a static, easily expressed concept. The correct answers were those that would allow her to get the job.

James brushed crumbs from his beard and led her ceremoniously into his bedroom which was dusty and drained of colour in daylight, a sad room in a way, that she'd only previously seen at night. The desk that had looked so lively, covered with notes and serious work, now seemed littered with half-finished projects. There was a tear in the corner of the D. H. Lawrence picture and the bed was soiled; when she moved the pillow she found an earring and held the piece of jewellery between her fingers, rubbing the silver circle back and forth.

'I won't feel guilty,' James cried, springing up. He told her he had to be free and whole, not dragged into the dirt of convention and dishonesty.

'Did she take all her clothes off?'

'Why do you ask such childish questions?' James said.

'So I can have the correct image in my mind. Tell me,' Alice begged.

James's lips expanded and contracted, shaping words she would remember later. Maddened by desire for her he'd settled for comfort in another. He pressed up against her, his anxious face above hers. 'You have to want me,' he said, his dark beard touching Alice's face. She stroked his eyelids and the tender skin under his eyes. His body was easy, like another limb, another self. 'Of course I want you,' she whispered.

'We'll go to the country,' James planned. Alice envisioned them lying in a green cave of grass. He held her face in his hands, kneeling in front of her. 'You're like a flower,' he moaned. This was really happening, Alice thought; her teacher was actually saying exactly what she'd thought about Wendy. On Saturday, they would take the ferry to his parents' place on Galiano Island, James told her tenderly as he walked her down the stairs and embraced her in the doorway. She noticed an old woman creeping along the sidewalk. James was delivering her from the possibility of becoming like that woman who carried a paper shopping bag marked by careful foldings and refoldings, saved in some drawer for dreary expeditions.

'I just wanted you to know Billy's in jail,' Wendy's voice cried bitterly when Alice answered the phone in the morning. 'You shouldn't have dumped him like that. The old guy he roughed up in the car charged him.'

Weren't there appeals or something? Parole? 'I didn't encourage him,' Alice heard her voice whine. She hoped her soul didn't contain invisible ice that froze men and caused them to destroy themselves.

'Well, it's too late now. He's in jail.'

'I only went out with him twice,' Alice reminded her friend.

'That's not the point,' Wendy stated flatly.

Beryl darted into the hall when Alice put down the phone. 'I hear you got fired,' she declared triumphantly. 'Don't think you're going to eat our food without contributing nothing, missy. Pawing that bearded creep and letting him feel you up and down. His father's the same as he is, his hand crawling up my leg at the dinner table with his stuck-up wife sitting there like butter wouldn't melt in her mouth,' Beryl yelled, gazing at Alice with hatred. 'You're not the only one the guys go for, you know. A mature woman has more sex appeal than a girl. Your boss says you don't even know how to work.'

There was a note on the refrigerator stating Alice should not eat anything.

CHAPTER NINETEEN

A WOMAN was supposed to supply lightness, lifting the man out of the dirt of life. If she got a job on Robson Street, James could stroll along the few blocks to where she worked and afterwards Alice imagined radiant conversations. She walked rapidly, glancing into windows in search of 'work wanted' signs and avoiding the eyes of men who lounged on street corners.

There was a notice stuck on the door of Rivers' Restaurant and Alice stepped into darkness and gazed at a large room filled with dim shapes. The restaurant was closed to customers until noon the sign on the door had said, but a large man emerged from the back and came towards her.

'I saw your notice,' Alice began, clasping her slippery purse in both hands.

The man's face was pale and floury but his head was topped by luxuriant waves of grey hair, as if vitality had flowed into this growth, bypassing his skin. 'You waitressed before?' he demanded suspiciously, his chin lifting pugnaciously, big arms hanging at his sides.

'Yes,' Alice lied.

'Be back at six and wear that dress,' the man ordered.

It was a black sundress she'd bought at the Army and Navy Store where the Woolworth's clerks often shopped on lunch hours. Alice strolled along the sidewalk, checking the reflection of this lucky garment in shop windows so she didn't notice Gordon until he snatched at her hand.

'Feed me,' he cried, waving his arms dramatically. 'I just went to the Unemployment Insurance Commission. They tried to tell me folk singing was a hobby.'

'What are you going to do?'

'Phone Mom. Don't look so shocked! James's mother gives him money, you know.'

'I don't think so, Gordon,' Alice said, worrying about the trip to Galiano with James. She was in a competition in which the finalists were Lady Chatterley and Ursula.

'You're an innocent.'

'I'm not,' Alice cried, insulted. 'What about James's mother?'

What annoyed Alice most was the knowledge that during her fateful appointment James would probably be watching her the whole time, wanting to know how she felt and checking on whether or not she was truly unselfconscious. What was important was the fusion of soul and body, self and other, into a fragile balance of completion and separation.

Gordon frowned as if trying to remember the details. '*You* know. Advances on his inheritance.'

They went to a matinée in a chilly theatre and afterwards sat in a little park covered with scrubby grass. 'We're the first generation that has had to face the reality of the Bomb,' Gordon sighed. 'Can I put my head in your lap?'

'No.'

Gordon rolled back. 'I thought not,' he said.

Light shimmered in the still air and the drone of traffic from Robson Street was muted. He told Alice he was about to make a dramatic change in his life, casting off his old existence. Instead of the impoverished troubadour, a young businessman would emerge. An uncle had offered him a job in his company and Gordon was planning to take it. Alice could scarcely believe Gordon's glib mouth was uttering such meek capitulation.

'I'm mediocre as a beat college dropout, my dear. I'm twenty-two.'

Alice hadn't realized Gordon was that old. After he became a businessman they would probably never meet again. She would be thinner and sexually experienced. Literature would rush through her brain like fever, consuming her.

'Do you judge me, dear Alice?' Gordon asked as they strode towards Rivers' Restaurant.

'Don't keep saying that, Gordon.' She stepped energetically beside him.

'And you've got a job, too,' Gordon commented.

'Only in a restaurant.'

'It sounds like a song, doesn't it?' Gordon sang the words.

Alice entered Rivers' Restaurant and made her way to the back table where the grey-haired man sat smoking a cigarette. The windows at the front were painted black and the tables were lit with candles flickering weakly in glass jars. A waitress with hot yellow hair ran back and forth balancing plates, a frown of concentration on her face.

His name was Leo, the grey-haired man said, and his partner, Nikos, grinned from the kitchen window where he presided over a steaming grill. The menu listed Greek, Italian and Canadian food.

'Isn't this a step down?' Mara asked Alice later in James's kitchen, but Alice scarcely noticed her words.

Mysterious Greek men gathered in the restaurant while she stepped between the tables, bearing steaming dishes. 'You look too delicate for this job,' one of the men had murmured and her pockets were heavy with tips.

Surrounded by soft night air, Alice and James strolled along the sea wall in Stanley Park, listening to waves splashing against the shore. Out on the dark water, lights floated on freighters waiting for a berth in the harbour, while on the far shore, quivering dots shone from the windows of houses and apartments in West Vancouver.

On the weekend, James reminded her, they would take the ferry and float across to Galiano. 'It's more beautiful than Greece,' he added.

'Your parents have a house there?' Alice asked. 'Really?' James often laughed when she mispronounced words she'd never heard spoken and now she worried he was joking, telling her a fairy tale about an island refuge where they'd cling together like lost children.

'Sure. A summer place.'

Her arm was wrapped around James's waist and she pressed her palm against him, trying to assess his possible level of tension or love. 'But I have to work on the weekend,' she explained. 'That's the restaurant's busiest time.'

'Jesus.' James stopped and grasped his head while his chest rose and fell with emotion. 'I can't take much more of this,' he cried.

Alice suppressed a nervous, guilty shudder. Sometimes James's reactions struck her as preposterous, but of course they weren't when examined from the point of view of the deep agonies of his soul. If she could only describe her situation clearly and completely she was sure his anger would leave him, but James interrupted her thoughts.

'I've had enough of that ultra-reasonable, mealy-mouthed tone,' he yelled. 'How dare you imply the fault is mine when you deny your own truth. This is an adolescent game you're playing! If you make claims to be a literate person you have to act like one and be judged like one.' He turned and ran across the damp grass into the shadows of some trees.

'But I didn't know when I made plans for a weekend with you that I'd get a job as a waitress,' she wailed into the darkness.

'I'm a man, Alice,' James's voice announced from a shadowy grove.

She stumbled after him calling his name tenderly but when she found him he leaned his face against a tree and wouldn't respond to her frantic explanations. Her own words struck her as feeble and lying and she wondered if she really was driven by unconscious, evil purposes. 'We can go another time,' she whispered, sickened by the possibility that she had a cold, duplicitous heart. Finally she walked back to the cement path alone, hoping he would run after her but he didn't.

'He was just using you,' Beryl commented when Alice stayed home in the evenings. 'I could have told you that. They stick with their own.'

Alice pictured James's face rapt with desire and love while he threaded his fingers through Mara's princess hair. She imagined James and Mara at parties where Mara's spoiled, petulant voice marked her as a loved, indulged woman. All James's friends would be delighted he'd dropped an unsuitable and somewhat absurd woman who mispronounced key words and had never been to Europe. In a paroxysm of rage and self-pity, Alice wandered back and forth through her mother's house while Beryl detailed her analysis.

'Lookit,' she said. 'His dad's a big cheese downtown. His son's going to marry a woman who can wear a white dress. Who'd marry you now?'

Alice turned the pages of the newspaper and looked at the photograph of a Vancouver reporter who'd won a prize for journalism. It was possible this woman might frequent one of the places James went and he'd be taken by her air of competence. She would laugh brazenly and his eyes would gleam. He would tell Gordon about the young, fascinating reporter and neither of them would remember Alice. James's life would rush ahead, rocketing into a thrilling future.

'You wouldn't listen to me,' Beryl sang out. 'So now you have to pay the price. You made your bed,' she cried. 'Now lie in it.'

Perhaps James had been secretly smirking with laughter at her clumsy manners and her odd remarks, Alice thought. He and Gordon might have rolled around on the gritty kitchen floor, laughing helplessly after she'd left. What if the whole relationship had been nothing more than a satirical skit in which she'd been unaware of her role as a comic player?

'You had your chance,' Beryl said.

Alice waited for the phone to ring or for James to appear in the doorway of the restaurant at closing. She found it difficult to believe that her fate should so quickly have become impossible. In a swoon of hopelessness she felt herself crumbling into meaningless fragments like Ozymandias, her unheard mouth hanging open. She saw Mara's avid face floating above her while she lay shattered like a traffic victim.

'Wake up,' Beryl advised.

Alice didn't like to leave her clothing in the bathroom because her mother studied it like a forensic scientist seeking a thread or stain indicating male emission. If anything was torn, Alice hid it at the back of her closet to avoid Beryl's theories about how the garment had been ripped from her daughter by a lustful man. One night Alice mended a gaping zipper while crouched in her bedroom, but she jumped up when she heard the ring of the telephone.

'She's not here,' Alice heard her mother state quietly.

'Yes I am,' Alice bounded out of the room to see Beryl setting the receiver back into its cradle.

'Who was it?' Alice stood in the hallway.

'Wrong number,' Beryl snapped, sauntering back into the living room.

'You didn't say that when you answered. You said *she* isn't here. Who's she?' Alice asked. What if it had been James? She couldn't call him. There was no getting around the fact that it was Mellors who followed Lady Chatterley to Venice.

Beryl squatted in her chair with her knees drawn up. 'What is this? The Gestapo? It was just some dame, probably drunk or something. Some nut, that's all.'

Alice's body grew hot with rage.

'Bertha Crumb, that's who she wanted,' Beryl said.

Alice clamped her hands to the sides of her head to prevent her skull from flying apart. 'Bertha Crumb!' she cried. 'No one has a name like Bertha Crumb!'

'Oh yeah?' Beryl shot back. 'That's what you think, Miss Know-It-All. I once knew a family named Crumb and a very nice family they were, too. Their daughter was a friend of mine.'

Tears of frustration sprang from Alice's eyes. 'That's why you thought of the name Crumb,' she wailed. 'Do you think I'm insane? Are you trying to drive me mad?'

'I don't have to drive you anywhere.' Beryl jumped up, banging against the little table so tea slopped over the edge of one of the cups and ran on to the floor in a beige rivulet. 'You're more and more nuts each day. You're mental. Maggie saw a whole TV programme about girls like you.'

'Like me?' Alice yelled.

'Hey! Quiet down,' Beryl cried. 'Boy-crazy girls to put it as nice as I can.'

The phone rang again and both women stared at each other, startled. Alice reached the telephone first and lifted the receiver but Beryl grabbed at the smeared black plastic, catching her fingers in Alice's hair.

'Give it here,' Beryl gasped.

Feet braced, Alice yanked at the phone, dragging her mother, but Beryl threw herself down and wrapped her body around the receiver, her face twisted with determination, while the base of the telephone thumped along the floor. Alice seized her mother's shoulders and pried at her fingers. 'You have no right to do this,' she panted.

Armadillo-like, Beryl rolled on the floor. 'You owe everything to me,' she cried furiously. 'I gave you life.'

Alice thought this was a disgusting idea. She'd heard people talk about returning to the womb, but the idea repelled her. Crawling on her hands and knees, she tried to see how she could get a firm grip on the older woman. As they struggled, Alice stared into her mother's blazing blue eyes and with a convulsive movement wrested the phone from her mother's grasp.

'Hello,' she called into the mouthpiece. 'Hello?'

'You bitch!' her mother shrieked, slapping helplessly at Alice while tears ran down her cheeks.

Alice slammed the receiver down when she heard the hum of the dial tone. 'Leave me alone,' Alice cried, smacking her open palm against the side of Beryl's head and the older woman stepped backwards, her expression shocked and frightened.

'You won't destroy me,' Alice screamed.

CHAPTER TWENTY

IT WAS nearly closing time in the restaurant when Alice noticed the sailor again. He'd been watching her for about a week, sitting alone while his shipmates shoved their tables together and sat in a loud group, speaking Greek and drinking from hidden bottles. She worried that he was an outcast, unhappily shut out by the other sailors; perhaps because he was middle-aged while they were young and full of high spirits, pounding on the tables to attract her attention when the restaurant was busy. However, she couldn't help it if the older sailor was unhappy she told herself firmly and refused all his requests to visit his ship on her day off. A youth with a mass of springy curls slipped a tanned arm around her waist and grinned proudly, encouraged by the shouts of his companions.

'More salad?' Nikos yelled cheerfully from the noisy kitchen when she gave him the sailors' order. Then the pay phone at the front of the restaurant rang and Alice hurried to answer it, picking up the receiver and turning to see Nikos peering through the window between the kitchen and the dining room.

'Is that you?' Beryl's voice was suspicious, attuned to the possibility of menace in the world.

'We've still got customers,' Alice said, keeping her eyes on the sailors who would soon sober up and become sullen and bad-tempered. She'd asked Beryl not to call the restaurant, pointing out that her mother could easily wait. However, driven by powerful impulses, Beryl continued to phone.

'I've really had it with Goldie,' her mother continued, speaking urgently. 'I'm getting rid of him.' Alice was silent, twisting the cord back and forth between her fingers. 'Are you still there?' Beryl demanded sharply. 'Are you asleep or something?

I'm going to be independent,' she announced. 'I called the welfare woman and she came over here today acting like some big shot psychiatrist. To hell with her! I'm getting the cheque tomorrow, anyways. I know how to work things.'

'Oh, yes!' Beryl exclaimed threateningly. 'There are going to be some changes around here! I'm going to do my whole bedroom Chinese! Bit by bit. That's really class, you know,' she snarled. 'I'm going to start with a fringed lampshade.'

'What about David?' Alice asked.

'Hey,' Nikos called. 'You can go now.'

Alice listened as her mother told her David's teachers objected to his odd clothing, the short, thick trousers Beryl found at the Salvation Army and the little flared coat with a worn, velvet collar. 'I dress him just like Prince Charles,' Beryl exclaimed, outraged. She said the teachers wanted the child to wear jeans and striped T-shirts similar to those of other pupils. 'I dress my child like the Queen's children,' Beryl had announced to the teacher while David hid in the cloakroom. 'Not like scum!' Alice moved the receiver gradually away from her ear and her mother's voice grew smaller but no less piercing.

When she left, Alice waved at Nikos, but none of the other men looked up; they would never leave a tip now. Her movements felt heavy and slow like those of someone trying to wade through deep water, but the next day she was buoyed up by Wendy's voice on the telephone saying she missed Alice and realized now that Billy was crazy. A prison doctor had examined him and told the family that Billy would have to take medicine for the rest of his life. 'Mum just doesn't get it,' Wendy added. 'Even though he's mental she's getting the whole church to pray for healing.'

Alice told Wendy about James.

'What a waste of young womanhood,' Wendy exclaimed loyally. 'Look around for somebody else. I'll ask Don if he can think of anyone.'

However Alice knew young womanhood had no particular value. Even Lawrence preferred older women. 'One human being can't be replaced with another,' Alice said sadly.

When the restaurant was opening, Alice picked matches and

cigarette butts out of the candles and filled the sugar containers, while Leo slumped at one of the tables near the women's washroom and smoked a cigarette. Nikos set out provisions in the kitchen and heated the grill, singing and poking his head through the window into the dining room occasionally.

Mara appeared in the doorway and sat at one of the tables, flopping her soft leather purse on to its surface. 'Water,' she said, miming unconsciousness. 'I'm exhausted. I've walked for miles.'

'Who is she? Some friend of yours? She can't come in here and just drink water,' Leo warned ferociously, his huge stomach rising and falling.

'What's this?' Mara asked, frowning at the menu Alice handed her. 'I just want something to drink. Do you have lemonade?'

'Seven-Up only,' Alice replied, wondering why she was speaking English like a second language, conscious of Leo and Nikos watching.

Mara gazed critically around the restaurant. 'I haven't seen you around and James won't say a word. What's going on?' she asked, laughing. She laid her white arms on the dark table, her pink mouth smiling slyly.

When she heard James's name Alice felt her body contract as though she'd been struck.

'You don't want to talk about it. Why should you?' Mara said pleasantly, laughing again and opening her handbag to extract a metal case filled with cigarettes. 'When these things are over there's just no point in drawing them out, is there?' Mara flicked her hand dismissively and rose from her chair. 'I was worried about you, that's all,' she called out as she left. Various scenes suggested themselves to Alice, complete with terrible dialogue. She almost groaned aloud when she pictured James's face registering polite pity at Mara's mention of her name.

That evening the older sailor returned, accompanied for the first time by companions: a man in a naval officer's uniform with braid on his cuffs and a woman in a tight white dress who had a darkly tanned face and pale blonde hair. When Alice approached to take their order, the woman spoke. 'George here,' she said, motioning towards the sailor, 'has been telling us he's invited you to see the ship.'

'Yes,' Alice confirmed warily.

'We'd like you to come too,' said the woman while the silent men stared up at Alice. 'This is Captain Vasilakos and I'm his fiancée, Barbara Marshall.'

Alice gave her name reluctantly, thinking Barbara seemed old to be anyone's fiancée; she was thirty at least and had large pores. It wasn't fair of them to pressure her to visit the ship. After all, she'd said no. She had no interest in ships. As far as she was concerned, they were simply large, boring, metal objects, usually grey. She'd be shown dials and meaningless shapes and even be told the names of these things. She didn't think she could stand it.

'Why don't you want to come?' Barbara demanded. 'Have you ever been on a ship before?' When Barbara asked about Alice's day off she gave the information unwillingly. Nikos was banging the kitchen bell, signalling her to pick up an order.

'Well then!' Barbara exclaimed with pleasure, looking around the table as if everything was settled. 'Why not come then?' The men regarded Alice intently. 'I'll be there,' Barbara added reassuringly. 'Is that it? Is that what's bothering you?'

'No,' Alice cried. She didn't want them to think that! She agreed to go before Barbara could say anything else.

'Good,' Barbara said briskly. Arrangements were made and Alice wrote the name of the ship on the back of her order pad and walked away, feeling doomed. She suspected most other people would look forward to seeing the ship and wondered if her own likes and dislikes were peculiar, even abnormal. She winced when cartoon characters exploded and at other times found herself laughing delightedly into a silence.

'Your mother phoned,' Nikos said later. 'How come she calls here all the time?'

Jeff was listening. He helped out in the kitchen when the restaurant was busy, but now he had finished his shift and leaned back in his chair. 'You're nineteen,' he offered. 'That's an adult. At least for a woman,' he added, grinning lewdly.

'Once in a while your mother should phone you. That's okay. But not every day!' He was a Canadian.

Nikos gave him a dirty look. 'Just tell her to phone late,' he advised.

After her shift was over, Alice returned her mother's call, dialling the familiar numbers and telling herself the conversation would soon be over. James could never understand why she hated her mother's telephonic intrusions. 'At least she's surprising,' he always said.

'Boy are you ever hard to get ahold of,' Beryl exclaimed. 'Goldie came around but I wouldn't let him in. David tried to open the door and I gave him an earful later. I've still got a good figure, you know. Once when I was at Maggie's, a friend of hers, a Polish girl or was it a Ukrainian?' Beryl paused, puzzled, and Alice could hear her mother drawing on a cigarette. 'I don't know. What's the difference,' she exclaimed crossly. 'Anyways, she said she sure hoped she'd have a figure like mine when she was forty.

'I bought a bikini today,' she continued. 'That's what they wear in France. David thought my stomach was too big or something. I didn't think it looked too bad but I returned it to that snob store. They told me no refunds but I shoved it right under the boss's nose and said, "See? It's never been worn." He gave me my money back all right!'

When Alice awakened on her day off she struggled out of sleep resentfully like a soul being called back, trying not to think of James and Mara or her mother thrashing and cursing through life like someone drowning. She shut out the images of Mr Goldman standing outside a closed door with David on the other side.

The sailor was waiting for Alice on the docks and as she walked ahead of him on the gangway she saw deep, black water beneath, scummed with oil and debris. She edged past giant spools wound with huge ropes and headed down a narrow, metal corridor where they entered a wood-panelled cabin.

Barbara smiled welcomingly. 'Drink?' she asked.

Alice sat demurely on her chair, refusing the offer and waiting for the tour of the ship. She was determined to be interested.

'Don't you drink?' Barbara asked sharply.

'Of course,' Alice assured her.

'Why don't you show her around the ship first?' Barbara proposed to the sailor who rose obediently and led Alice down the narrow corridor again. Alice wished she could remember his name as they trudged through clanging passages into grey, metal rooms filled with silent machines and motionless dials. To demonstrate her good will to the lonely, displaced Greek, Alice beamed at him and at whatever machinery he pointed out, though her thoughts were swarming with memories of James. In the wheelhouse she stared at a pastel portrait of Jesus holding a ship's wheel in his aristocratic hands.

'Christos,' explained the sailor.

'Yes,' she agreed as they stood and contemplated the picture.

Suddenly the sailor burst out, 'You look like Greek girl,' and grabbed Alice, clamping her to his chest.

What did he mean? thought Alice distractedly. That she looked Greek? That she had unwittingly given some signal that had inflamed his passion? They stood locked and immobile until he unclasped his arms and led her back to the captain's cabin without a word. In a fury, Alice followed his thick body through labyrinthine corridors to the cabin where a table was unfolded from the wall and a cabin boy rushed in with trays heaped with steaming prawns. The captain poured a glass of Ouzo for her and she sipped desperately at the burning liquid while waiting for an opportunity to leave politely even though her chest burned with rage. It wasn't Barbara's fault the sailor was untrustworthy.

'You must drink it,' Barbara urged. 'Otherwise, they'll be offended because it's their national drink.' Alice's lips were tight against the rim of the tumbler.

Without warning, the captain seized the glass and pushed it against her mouth. 'Drink!' he shouted, holding her chin firmly but Alice sat stiffly with her mouth stubbornly shut.

'Don't force her! Don't force her!' Barbara cried, waving her hands as if fearing for the success of her party.

The captain turned away impatiently while the sailor pushed

himself up, announced he was leaving and marched out. Alice watched the cabin door swing shut.

'I'll be right back,' Barbara sang out. 'I'm just going to the washroom.' She too slipped away.

Alarmed, Alice stood up but the blue serge arms of the captain closed around her. 'You look like a girl in Greece!' he exclaimed. 'Maria! I have a picture.' He held Alice tightly against his domed metal buttons.

Could there possibly be some Greek look-alike inspiring all this passion? Alice asked herself, pulling away from him.

'No, no,' he remonstrated, explaining again that she looked like Maria and adding something about love and Greece. Finally, he unclasped her and stepped back, continuing to speak placatingly.

Alice fled through an aperture and rapped on the metal door of the toilet which was quickly opened by Barbara. When Alice burst in the captain followed her so all three stood wedged in the narrow cubicle.

'What's wrong?' Barbara asked.

Alice was conscious of being surrounded by metal walls. The captain had closed the door behind him and his body blocked the exit. She had always snickered when Beryl talked about young women disappearing but now she wondered if these stories might be true.

'What's the matter?' Barbara's face appeared puzzled. 'Would you like to make love while I instruct? Or we could make love while he watches,' Barbara suggested, bringing her face tentatively forward while Alice pressed back against the wall.

'It's no use,' Barbara informed the captain at last. 'She doesn't want to. She's scared.'

They filed out of the washroom and Alice picked up her purse in a daze. Then the sailor appeared and led her to the dock where she called a taxi from a direct-line telephone attached to a weathered post. Alice turned away from him, wondering if some signal might still be given at which she'd be hurled into the oily water. The sailor stood silently at her side but as the cab pulled up he burst out, 'You not business girl. I love you! I want to marry you!'

At Rivers', Alice picked up her cheque and cashed it so she could pay Beryl for room and board, but as she was leaving a group of Canadians signalled her to their table. They wanted to settle an argument and she turned reluctantly, recognizing one of them, a young man with a thin face who often came to the restaurant.

'Listen,' one of the men said. 'What would you do if a criminal,' he paused for a moment, 'someone who had done something really terrible, came into the restaurant and gave you a beautiful bouquet of flowers? What would you do?' The men regarded her steadily.

Alice imagined herself wiping the tables and the criminal sauntering in with flowers wrapped in thin green paper. He'd done some ugly thing, killed someone perhaps, or maimed somebody, but now he was in a good mood and wanted her affection. He wanted to tell her he really hadn't been himself when the terrible things had happened. He'd been weak, just for a moment, or angry. He'd lost control. He held out the flowers timidly, like a child.

'I'd throw up!' she responded, looking defiantly at the men. The criminal thought all he had to do was give her flowers and everything would be all right. But it wasn't. The men regarded her uneasily. Alice knew she was supposed to say something forgiving and understanding and mealy-mouthed, but she wasn't going to do it. Instead, she would choose a world where actions were determined by fervent love and fearless ideals. She'd been a fool, she said to herself as she hurried through the back lanes to James's house. She told him she was trying to escape shoddy evils committed by people staggering through life in a trance of unconsciousness.

'But that's the only kind of consciousness that matters,' James cried as she walked into his room. 'All else is mere cerebration.'

She told him about the ship, how the sailors ran ratlike along corridors, diminished by the vastness of their metal pen floating on the sea. Ouzo was as clear as water but it tasted thick, like poison.

'You have such adventures,' he said admiringly. 'Nothing like that ever happens to me.'

She saw he was taken by the drama of her sudden, unexpected arrival and the intensity of her demeanour. This knowledge made her feel more powerfully female, invincible and daring, so she unzipped her dress and tossed it on a chair while he gazed at her, amazed. In his narrow bed she held him while his thin chest rose and fell, gasping as if he were in pain. Was love torn out of him? she wondered. Did it cause him suffering?

'Of course not,' he told her later when she asked. 'Delight.'

Alice called Beryl and told her she was spending the night at Wendy's. In the morning the shopkeeper at the corner store rang up a stick of butter, a loaf of bread and a jar of imported jam while she and James smiled secretly to each other. When they ate, James licked her buttery fingers and later he dropped the extra housekey into her purse.

CHAPTER TWENTY-ONE

THAT EVENING Beryl stood silently at the sink in the kitchen, rattling the dishes in soapy water when Alice returned from work.

'Where's David?' Alice asked.

'That's for me to know and you to find out,' Beryl replied crisply, her back tense.

'Is he with Mr Goldman?' Alice persisted. Beryl had told the social worker David's father was unknown so she could take Mr Goldman's money as well as the government cheque.

'There's a sandwich on the table,' Beryl stated. 'Eat it and get out. If you're not back by eleven I'll phone the police and have you put in reform school. I called your whore-friend and she didn't know nothing about where you were last night.'

'I'm a bit old for the reformatory,' Alice remarked as she pushed a piece of bread and boloney into her mouth at the kitchen table.

'I can put two and two together,' Beryl yelled.

Afterwards Alice wandered through streets that were like a maze filled with repetitious shapes. Let her not phone James, Alice prayed fervently, flooded with tenderness at the thought of him because he was so lovely with his dissatisfied frown, his delicate, knobbly chest and his dark, vital beard.

When she returned she drifted down the hall to her room and opened her closet to discover it contained only a pair of baby-doll pyjamas on a metal hanger. Even the shoes had gone. She slid out her dresser drawers quietly but they too were empty. Pondering this new situation, Alice sat on the side of her bed. Obviously Beryl had prepared a shocking lesson, but Alice's heart felt like a stone within her chest, heavy and painful with stubborn resolve. In the other room, her mother waited for her reaction, expecting sobbing repentance perhaps; instead, Alice coldly took off her clothes and folded them in a pile on the dresser. She donned the thin nylon pyjamas and slid into the cold bed, dreaming as she slept of beetles swarming across the floor and crawling on to the blanket.

'Get up and get out,' Beryl hissed into Alice's ear in the morning and Alice opened her eyes to view her mother's oily skin close to her own cheek.

'I want you out of here before David wakes up,' Beryl ordered. 'And leave the money you owe me on the table.'

When her mother left the room Alice pulled on her things, her hands clumsy with buttons and zippers.

'You can make one phone call,' Beryl announced, standing wrapped in her dressing gown in the living room.

Through the window Alice could see it was still dark but there was a line of light on the horizon. Wondering if her mother had learned her speeches from police shows on television, Alice lifted the receiver and Beryl disappeared into her bedroom, shutting the door. Outside the streets were empty of cars, the grass, soaked in dew and the porch, shadowy and damp. On the top step Alice found a couple of cardboard cartons tied with cord and she pulled up a flap to see her clothes inside, neatly folded. Astounded at this exhibition of her mother's organization and skill, Alice dragged the boxes to the sidewalk and waited for the sound of the taxi. It was all strangely like a dream, she thought, in which a bright yellow car stops beside a young woman and she jumps into the cab and sits on the plastic seat, staring straight ahead, while she holds in her mind the picture of the chill house behind her: David curled in sleep with his small hands relaxed on the blanket, the lines of his fate etched on his palm.

At James's house on Thurlow, Alice opened the door carefully with the key he'd given her, struggled up the stairs with her boxes and slid them into a corner. James emerged sleepily from the bedroom, his hair sticking out in tufts and his face shocked and young.

James embraced her. 'God,' he said when she explained. 'Your life is like a confession magazine or something.' He was leaving in a few days for a conference on Lawrence where he was to give a paper based on his thesis.

'We'll live together,' James exclaimed, pulling at his beard. 'We won't be controlled by the death-loving customs of this society. We've gone beyond that.'

When he told her about the conference he said jousting for power was exhilarating. She was the one who gave him strength and vigour, especially important now because this was his début as an academic, his very first paper. His outside examiner, an eminent professor named Porter would be there, the only one James feared. Alice listened, wanting James to tell her how happy he was to have her stay, but she knew he hated insecurity in women. Feminine weakness could emasculate a man; she was to be the fertile base from which James could spring up in his full power.

Living with Alice gave James a certain cachet in his group and his kitchen became a popular salon. The men pronounced Alice more womanly and wise than their own girlfriends and she learned to make huge pots of chilli and Spanish rice. While the company held forth on art and life, Alice served sour rye bread and thin slices of cheese from a German delicatessen. Her remarks were thought to be fresh and interesting. The men quoted Alice to their girlfriends, exclaiming that she believed in struggling against fate.

James began to be consulted as an authority and discussions about Lawrence went on until morning. Alice bought a large candle and set it on the table so the men's eyes glittered in the darkness as they divided the universe into the quick and the dead. Sometimes, when Alice had to work an early shift in the restaurant, she went to bed before they left and the men filed into the room to kiss her good-night.

She was entranced by these men who were amusing and gentle with their large hands and faces. There were many things they couldn't do and if a geyser shot out of the bathroom plumbing they had to call for Alice and huddle in the doorway while she rattled bits of metal in the tank. They found it impossible to find things in the cupboards or the refrigerator yet they could quote poetry and discuss obscure subjects at length. She loved their masculine movements, their bodies which were full of energy and strength. One of them, a man from Montreal, had thick blond hair that crackled with energy, like a yellow animal on his head, and he claimed to have smoked marijuana obtained from genuine beatniks. Alice questioned him about this drug even though James warned her that smoking reefer was the act of a dead soul seeking final annihilation. James said human beings were less spontaneous than animals because, unlike them, people were burdened with memory. This meant people were less alive even than sea-urchins.

'Consider the sea-urchin,' he cried, 'how it opens itself to life, exposing itself like a flower.'

When Alice did the laundry she folded James's garments carefully, charmed by their foreign shapes and manly size. She patted his turtleneck T-shirts, so wonderfully imbued with maleness.

'Whore,' Beryl yelled when Alice picked up the telephone in the restaurant. 'You're headed down,' she screamed. 'Dirt finds its own level. Goldie's disgusted.'

Mr Goldman's brother-in-law had called Beryl saying Mr Goldman was lonely and painful emotion was bad for his heart. Mr Goldman planned to sell the laundromat and retire in a couple of years and then there would be more money, Ben promised. Besides, there was the boy.

'I've taken him back,' Beryl announced cosily. 'After all the poor old bugger can't have many years left. There's peace and quiet around now you're gone so it's a better place for him. I let Ben know what you're up to. You can be sure of that.'

Now that she was free of Beryl whose voice could only come threading through telephone wires, Alice decided to see Mr Goldman in his laundromat. The moist, warm air closed around her when she entered the small launderette where machines chugged pleasantly and she could smell the faint blue odour of cigar smoke underneath the scent of detergent. At the back, Mr

Goldman sat on a metal chair and held a crossword puzzle book open to a page he'd almost finished marking neatly in blue ink.

As she walked in she could feel words rising up in her, language that would describe truth so accurately that Mr Goldman's protective instincts would be roused and he'd utter some manly dictate that would cause her mother to repent. Beryl was an emotional guerrilla, jumping out to inflict wounds and sinking back into the terrain as if nothing had happened at all. Mr Goldman would soon be able to see this clearly. Yet when they greeted each other and Mr Goldman dusted off the chair next to him, motioning for Alice to sit, it pained her to see his scalp looking naked and old so she kept silent.

'What's that book you're reading?' Mr Goldman asked and Alice declared it was about transcendence. 'It's important to have a good vocabulary,' he responded while Alice admired his noble profile and his air of sad resignation.

A woman in a red convertible parked her car out front and ran to drag her laundry from the dryer. 'Goodbye, Mr Goldman,' she cried cheerily as she plunged out with the heavy basket. She was a plump woman in tight red pants and her blonde hair was wrapped around curlers and tied with a spangled scarf. It had never occurred to Alice before that Mr Goldman had a life, that each day he observed women folding their intimate belongings. The blonde woman waved and drove off with her spangles glittering in the sun.

'Are you sure you understand all these books you read?' Mr Goldman asked.

'Of course,' Alice cried. It was ordinary life that was difficult to comprehend, not literature. After a pause, she announced that she couldn't live at home any more, enjoying the drama of her statement. 'Beryl and I don't get along,' Alice explained. Wasn't that a wonderfully mild way of stating the problem? she thought.

'From what your mother tells me, you're quite a prevaricator now,' Mr Goldman answered.

'I don't know what that means,' Alice said. It was humiliating to present herself as someone who understood literature and then ask for the definition of a word, but that was her new policy. James said only uneducated people lacked the confidence to say they didn't know something.

'A liar, if you know what I mean,' Mr Goldman said sternly, crossing one leg over the other.

At work afterwards her fingers were slow and she had to marshal all her will to hold on to the dishes. She grieved as she ran with hot platters of mixed grill and spaghetti. The word must have formed in Mr Goldman as soon as he saw her enter the laundromat and he only waited for an opening to deliver its poison. She was tormented by the thought that she'd caused Mr Goldman to deviate from his true nature of courtly refinement and sensitivity, his gift for unspoken love. Once lies had been told by Beryl their power could never be reduced. She should have known that.

At James's, Gordon was standing in the kitchen, looking into the empty cupboards when she came through the door. James was still out at the university, working in his office.

'Women are very odd, Alice,' Gordon said. 'Except you, of course.' He pulled out an oval tin of anchovies. 'What are these?' he asked querulously.

'Small, strong-tasting fish,' Alice replied, placing her feet up on the seat of the opposite chair. She could tell that this was one of those conversations in which Gordon would seem helpless while she would appear wise. 'What's wrong?' she asked.

'My lady-friend,' Gordon sighed.

Alice nodded but the centre of her chest was tight with sorrow and humiliation. She saw herself wandering into Mr Goldman's laundromat, a novel in her hand to demonstrate her spiritual kinship with him.

'Do you want me to make you some tea?' Alice asked. 'And cinnamon toast?' Mr Goldman was too tender to withstand Beryl's harshness and too fine to comprehend duplicity.

'Yes. Take care of me,' Gordon said weakly. 'God knows I need some womanly attention. Do we have egg bread?'

Alice sliced through the spongy, golden bread, watching as the knife moved inexorably through the cells of air, unstoppable, despite the delicacy of the structures it destroyed. She slipped the slices into the sides of their old toaster and waited to turn them. The wires glowed red as she warmed her hands.

'You have pretty legs,' Gordon said suddenly.

'Gordon!'

'Men are beasts, I'm afraid,' Gordon pronounced, leaning back in his chair in a lordly manner as Alice put the plate of toast on the table. 'Food soothes the soul,' he exclaimed. 'Especially toast, have you noticed that? Cut into little triangles.' He crammed the sweet, crisp bread into his mouth.

After work she usually came home to a kitchen full of cigarette smoke, dishes and men. This revivifying scene provided her with proof she'd escaped her mother's grasp at last. Education was the thing that could drag a person out of any misery and lift her into a world of marvels. She tossed her tips into a green Chinese bowl and they used the money for food, running with handfuls of coins to the little store on Robson to buy provisions for late night feasts. They had to have chocolate covered biscuits and fresh strawberries in the evening and in the morning they consumed purple grapes and German cheese. No one ate the orange cheddar Alice had been brought up on, James said.

She made a list of her favourite words and the others joined in, calling out words like languor to be savoured and discussed late into the night. Although she mourned Mr Goldman, she knew this was her true family.

CHAPTER TWENTY-TWO

JAMES SWIVELLED AROUND from his desk. 'We're late,' he said. The floor was covered with crumpled pages, representing false starts on the last chapter of his thesis.

Alice moved a piece of paper away from the burning tip of the cigarette smouldering in the ashtray beside him and pulled off her white apron with its saucy bow. 'I know,' she admitted undoing the buttons that ran down the front of her black uniform. 'I just got off work.' Pacing back and forth in a creative rapture, James gestured grandly and talked while she hung a strand of coffee beans around her neck like the ones she'd seen Phillipa Kirke wear. Alice interrupted James when he complained that his mother had tried to keep him in blood bondage to her.

'You're free of that now,' she assured him. He had sudden collapses of confidence during which he asked her to list all the factors that would lead to his freedom and success and Alice was riveted with the importance of her task. 'Am I?' he murmured, clasping her against the pens bristling from his breast pocket. They were expected at a party at Phillipa's large house, a splendid dwelling that had been part of a divorce settlement, a relic from a painful episode in which Phillipa's husband, an art history professor, had run off with one of his students.

'Don't be so shocked,' James said. 'Lawrence did the same sort of thing. He chose a woman who left her children to be with him.'

'Maybe Lawrence didn't realize what the outcome would be,' Alice remarked in the bus taking them to the university endowment lands.

'Are you kidding? Whatever anyone might say about Lawrence, he was above any mawkish denial of reality,' James responded. The bus swerved around Blanca Loop where they had to transfer. It was very dark and though Alice had imagined there would be a glorious stone entrance to the university, perhaps chiselled with noble sentiments in Latin, she could see nothing but trees and blackness. In the smeared window of the second bus she regarded her own face staring back at her, appearing tired and frighteningly plain. Daunted by this apparition, she trotted beside James when they got out and headed down a long street, where round globes shone like pale moons through the leaves. Dizzy with foreboding, Alice clung to James's hand. Phillipa was a patron of the arts, he told Alice, and visiting poets and painters stayed at her house when they came to town. He guided Alice up a curved walk edged with frondy pampas grass.

Uttering a cry of welcome, Phillipa flung open the door. Behind her, Professor Wilson, the thin older man Alice had noticed at James's party, leaned against a large, abstract statue in the entrance hall while ashes fell from his cigarette on to the polished floor. James had said the man was very modern and progressive, despite his age.

Noting Phillipa's wonderfully thin arms and her heavy silver earrings, Alice felt herself becoming a plump bundle scurrying past into the crowded living room, throwing herself quickly into a basket chair. The room was lit with a multitude of candles, shining on to the faces and bodies of guests. It was like a film, Alice thought, in which every person and object had been selected for aesthetic reasons. Impressed, she walked through an arched doorway to a table covered with Mexican dishes containing artistically arranged food. A woman was scooping some on to her plate.

This woman was dressed in a long, shimmering tunic of Indian silk, its colours changing from bronze to green in the light. 'Aren't these irresistible?' she cried, seizing a stuffed mushroom between her fingers, pushing it into her mouth and chewing ecstatically.

'Do I know you?' she inquired, brushing off her hands. She

shoved her plate on to a corner of the table, so it smacked against a platter of prawns.

'I'm Alice Mallory,' Alice said, ready in case the woman sprang forward in some kind of greeting.

Arching her brows, the woman stretched her mouth open, turned her head towards the man at her side and then stared at Alice. 'Should that mean something?' she called out. 'I've never heard of you,' she cried, laughing.

'I thought I would say my name and then you would say yours,' Alice burst out. Afterwards, she berated herself for gaucherie and wormlike humility. The woman glistened like a goddess and somehow the conversation turned to locations of note, none of which had been visited or inhabited by Alice. 'Paris? Berlin? London?' the woman asked, exasperated, and when another couple cried joyfully and embraced the shining woman, Alice returned to the living room and sat on a low, severe couch. On the opposite wall was a huge painting, violent with colour.

'Young Alice,' Professor Wilson cried, easing himself on to the sofa beside her. 'My flower-faced girl.'

James was still talking to Phillipa and they were joined by a man with dark hair and a sullen demeanour who wore a black leather jacket and stood with hands thrust into his pockets.

'Alice wandering through the underworld,' the professor sighed. 'Beware, poor Alice.'

'Am I in danger?' Alice asked lightly, looking away from his old man's hand closing on her arm. Across the room someone was trying to switch on a black pole lamp.

'In stories young girls walk through dangers they overcome, but in life the opposite is true,' Professor Wilson said. 'Life isn't like literature.'

How sad that this man, perhaps through terrible disappointments or the ravages of drink, should have come to such a wrong-headed position, Alice thought. Time and biology were so unrelenting. He had once actually been young, she supposed, and capable of sex and love. He must still retain some recollection of that time, like Adam's and Eve's memory of a lost, paradisal garden.

James crouched on the floor beside the couch and whispered into Alice's ear, telling her the man in the black jacket was a poet from the East Coast.

'You *have* to dance with me,' Mara insisted, pulling James up and leading him away.

Alice was shocked to see James participate in an ordinary activity just like a regular person, despite his great gifts. Then another couple leapt into the centre of the room, pressing their bodies together, groaning, and calling out, 'Oh, God!' They doubled up with laughter and another pair joined them, kissing each other and shrieking, 'I never knew it could be like this!'

Alice watched James's face as he gripped his pipe between his teeth, shoving his hands into the pockets of his dark brown corduroys, staring at the floor, the crests of his brows drawn together in a frown. His lips worked at his pipestem as bluish plumes of smoke drifted upwards.

People resumed conversations when the foursome rushed out of the room. The leather-jacketed poet leaned one arm on the mantel. Alice noticed people didn't dance much, preferring, she supposed, the elegant movements of language to the lurchings of the body, and being wonderfully absorbed in themselves; opening their mouths often to display perfect teeth and tossing back glossy hair. She sat at the edge of the room, seeing herself a member of an audience, viewing the universe of happy, interesting people caught up in celebration of themselves.

Phillipa bounded on to a low table and stood jauntily above them all, stretching out her arms like a priestess. She wanted to credit the muses who'd inspired her recent poems, she proclaimed, and when someone handed her a goblet she downed its contents while her friends applauded.

'She says I'm her muse,' Professor Wilson told Alice, flopping his head on to her shoulder, 'but she betrayed me by moving away from the vital speech of the common man. Never trust her,' he warned. 'When you've lived for sixty years like I have you see the commerce of art. Yet even a vixen's gift is better than nothing.'

Sixty! Alice was thinking. And yet he still laid his head hopefully upon a strange girl's shoulder at a party.

'Art and love,' Professor Wilson moaned, reaching across Alice's chest. 'That's all there is.'

'That's enough,' James cried, yanking Alice up.

'James,' Alice said. 'Don't.'

Professor Wilson's rheumy eyes filled with tears. 'Oh, how foolish,' he said, kicking at a wine bottle that spun off across the floor. Men gathered, soothing Professor Wilson and leading James away.

Hiding from the gaze of strangers, Alice stepped on to the porch and shut the door behind her, waiting for James to discover her; a pensive, perhaps even mysterious, figure. The night grew colder and she heard shrieks and laughter coming from the house but no one appeared in the silent garden. From Phillipa's porch Alice could see the lights of North Vancouver across the inlet. When the door opened finally, light fell in a patch on to the wooden deck and Alice was certain James would embrace her and stroke her cold arms, but instead a couple appeared, clasped together like gargoyles. The woman shrieked, 'There's someone just sitting there in the dark!'

Alice fled down the pale cedar stairs, past white flowers in a stone container, past the pampas grass. She was too weak, too frail and slow of thought for the bright, lively people at Phillipa's party. On the bus that raced along the dark boulevard and tore down the hill towards the city, she sat alone. Later, she was sure, James would say he regretted the distractions that caused him to leave her unattended and perhaps mention the remarkable quality of their love, how it was different from the ordinary kind, more rare and profound. When he said such things she felt marvellously peaceful, but now she sprang from the bus and strode quickly under the arched branches of trees towards Michael Halek's house where she saw the lights were on.

Michael opened the front door when she knocked, ushering her into a pleasant front room where students' assignments were spread out on an oak table. 'I've been at a party,' Alice said, ignoring the handsome ginger tom-cat rubbing at her ankles, trying to describe Phillipa's so Michael could see the perfect food arranged on beautiful plates beside a pyramid of wine glasses (real ones, not paper cups), the pure, clear sound of the hifi, the predatory faces of the guests and the bullying artwork. 'Grace and beauty can be bought,' Alice complained.

'What do you expect?' Michael asked. He stroked the cat that had jumped into his lap. 'These people are bourgeois pragmatists competing for economic and social gain. They're neo-aristocrats,' he said. 'They're determined to possess all advantages, access to the finest art, music and so on.'

'What are my choices?' Alice wailed. Only the exalted language of intellectuals, she was sure, could utter the heart's secrets. 'Whatever their faults, these people are connected to ideas and meaning.'

'I'm afraid you have a romantic sensibility,' Michael remarked, shaking his head. 'You underestimate the power of the material world, the force of social conditions.'

Alice took this as a compliment and lit a cigarette, breathing in the drugging smoke.

'It's dangerous to seek the sublime,' he added. 'And it indicates a distaste for reality. You're much too attracted to the glamour of metaphysical ideas.'

Alice sat back in her chair carelessly, crossing her legs. Michael didn't understand the bohemian world in which things like class didn't really matter since people recognized only those things that were important, true and profound. Beggars and scholars could converse about philosophy, art and life. Michael just wasn't a member of this intellectual vanguard so Alice tried to explain her living situation to him.

'How much do James and Gordon contribute to this arrangement?' he asked sternly.

Michael had seized upon the least relevant aspect. What did money matter? Impatiently, Alice put out her cigarette. 'We share things,' she explained. She looked around the room which had a bare, hardwood floor and white walls where a few Japanese prints hung in narrow, black frames. Later she sat terrified and laughing on Michael's knees as they rushed down a hill, the wheels of his chair flashing in the light from the streetlamps. James was in bed asleep when she entered the bedroom with her hair wild.

'Where were you?' he whimpered, his face very young. 'I was terribly worried. What happened?'

'I went to visit Michael,' Alice whispered.

'You're such a free spirit,' he murmured in his child's voice, falling back into the warm safety of sleep.

CHAPTER TWENTY-THREE

'I THINK I'll go to Italy first,' Mara exclaimed. 'Or maybe France. Oh, I don't know,' she laughed, jingling her heavy bracelets. 'I wish I were like you, Alice, living life at subsistence level with everything primitive and forbidding, but I just don't have that intensity to motivate me.' She glanced from James to Gordon. 'I envy you. I really do. I'm so spoiled.'

Alice pressed her back on to the living-room floor and angled her feet up on the wall. She'd just finished a double shift and she'd brought home a Greek salad which James and Gordon were consuming while offering advice about Mara's approaching trip to Europe. James, who had often pronounced Mara a very silly woman, now told her she harped on in a brittle, modern way that was absolutely deathlike, so Alice was surprised when he agreed to walk Mara to the bus stop.

'Don't you mind?' Gordon asked when the pair thudded down the stairs to the street. The house was full of echoes and reverberations; when anyone took a bath the pipes knocked and clanged within the walls.

'I trust James,' Alice said serenely, pleased she wasn't worried any more by base notions about human nature. A person in love released his or her hold on such ignoble ideas. James had told her he'd never been in love before so it was as if he was newly created, sinless. 'I'm your Adam,' he'd murmur. 'Besides,' she added practically to Gordon, 'if he and Mara were going to have an affair, don't you think they would have had one by now?'

James returned quickly and when Gordon left the room, carrying the tray aloft, James put his mouth next to Alice's ear and told her that Mara had grabbed him and kissed him.

'I was shocked,' he said. 'She gave me a big, wet kiss and said I was her favourite friend, the only one she'd be sorry to leave.'

Alice thought his confession had the same quality as her confidences to Wendy – simple, amazed reporting of events requiring interpretation. She was James's best friend, she realized, but as she caressed him she was bewildered by the way Mara, so stylish and assured, could press sudden kisses upon James's lips.

'James,' Alice called out in the morning. She leaned back on her elbows, still in bed. 'How much money do you get from your grant?'

'What a lot,' she commented when he told her.

'You have no idea what things cost,' James answered, knotting his new tie. 'I have to look presentable, you know. People are looking me over and everything depends on how I handle myself.'

Alice was consumed by a desire to comfort him, to smooth away the crease between his eyebrows and to offer wise comment. She'd noticed he'd recently bought clothing from Edward Chapman and had purchased professorial glasses, but she hadn't understood the significance of these acquisitions. Though burdened by manly worries, he'd tried to spare her and she'd upset him on the very morning he was leaving for an important conference.

'What are conferences really like?'

'You'd hate them,' James grinned, tossing clean socks and underwear into his suitcase. 'You're superior to all that posturing.'

Alice leaned back on the pillow. 'Don't go,' she called out childishly, holding up her arms.

'I wish I could stay here with you,' he whispered, kneeling beside her in his pressed trousers and tweed jacket. His woven tie drifted across her chest and his beard was still damp from the shower. She hugged him to her breast feeling the rasp of tweed on her bare arms. He would get a job and take her with him to a grassy campus where they'd attend concerts and watch foreign films. The walls of their house would be covered with shelves of books. Her mother wouldn't be able to figure it out, but Mr Goldman would be quietly approving when she and James took David with them on holidays abroad.

In the shower, she watched water run in sheets over her body as she admired her perfect skin, unmarked by age. She would never be one of those tired, drooping women. There was no need for that, she thought, stepping briskly out of the tub and rubbing herself with a towel which was actually hers and James's, enjoying the comforting plurality of ownership and the future it implied.

'Listen,' Alice's mother commanded when she telephoned the restaurant that night. Now that Mr Goldman had returned she couldn't bear his presence. He spent more time with her than ever, Beryl hissed. 'The other day he asked me if I'd seen his glasses anywhere and I looked around the place and guess where they were? Rolled up in a pair of pajamas. He's not all there! Oh, I know you've got a soft spot for him but you don't know what he's like.' Her voice outlined Mr Goldman's faults. He wanted to read in bed at night, preventing Beryl from enjoying her TV programmes, because the light coming from under the bedroom door irritated her eyes while she sat in the dark living room. The knowledge that behind the closed door he was turning pages, tormented her; she was certain she could hear their rhythmic rustle. The gleam of his scalp was more than she could endure.

Alice reached into the pocket of her apron and fingered the slippery coins customers had left on the tables.

'He could live for years, you know,' Beryl continued. 'That's what Maggie says. David's always on Goldie's side, of course.' She gulped liquidly and Alice immediately saw her mother gripping the pale mug, gleaming with its sickening coating of iridescence.

Leo yawned and switched on the overhead lights, revealing the tables and floor, once covered in mysterious darkness, to be smeared and filthy, strewn with soiled napkins and cigarette butts.

'What are you sniffing about?' Beryl demanded.

'I have a cold,' Alice said. Outside the restaurant, rain fell steadily and the sidewalks were covered with wet, mashed leaves.

'Yeah? Big deal. You don't have to sound like you're dying,' Beryl jeered. 'I always worked when I was sick and you didn't hear me complain.'

'I AM working,' Alice reminded her mother.

'Sure. As soon as I tell you about my problems all of a sudden you're sniffing and snuffing. You want all the attention on you. Well, don't think you're going to come home at Christmas and poison David's mind and turn him into a bum like you.'

With great concentration, Alice folded the sleeve of her sweater into a perfectly even cuff. 'Is this all because I sneezed?' she demanded.

Cringing from cold, Alice hurried past the closed shops on Robson while rain soaked her hair and ran into her mouth. Some of the stores already had tinsel in their windows and expensive objects nestled in puffs of angel hair. Alice remembered handling this substance at Woolworth's and the irritation caused by its brittle fibres. She intended to ward off seasonal gloom, the descent of unattractive torpor, because she knew she held James only by the fragile spell of her charm. Though he said she was beautiful, it was not an accurate assessment; his perception resulted from the enchantment of what he saw as her exotic background and the uneducated freshness of her remarks.

'I have a knack for connecting seemingly incoherent bits of information in a startling way,' she told Michael. 'So what? It's a parlour trick.' She feared being put aside like an animal whose antics had become repetitive and boring. She was not like James's friends, truly grasping various branches of knowledge, steeped in history and ancient languages.

Michael groaned. 'They aren't like that either,' he told her, exasperated by her ideas. 'You think intellectuals are better people than waitresses and clerks,' he cried. 'Do you notice you grabbed the first academic you met?'

'That was just a coincidence,' Alice said. 'He wasn't just the first academic. He was the first person I'd ever known who'd read D. H. Lawrence.' She was wearing an old, black sweater of James's that he'd given her and she wrapped her arms around herself, touching the fine wool. 'I just don't want endless ugliness and brutality,' she said, wishing James were back from his conference. Even though he described academia as a barnyard, where men displayed brains instead of feathers to gain the power and recognition they needed to win the best females, he was forced to participate, despite his perception and sensitivity, simply because he lived in an imperfect world.

'There are subtle forms of brutality too,' Michael warned, but Alice ignored his comment. 'Stylish violence,' he added.

She was asleep when James returned from the conference and she opened her eyes to see him gazing at her tenderly. She began to tell him about her dream but he only said, 'Hold thy tongue, woman, and let me love.' Afterwards he showed her a photograph of Professor Porter and she saw that the great man had a tiny, cranky face like an elf.

He was a difficult person, according to James, who said joyfully that the famous professor was not at all staid. Once Professor Porter had even been enticed to give a talk at a certain university by an attractive female student who was sent by the English Department for that purpose.

'There's a pimp that comes into the restaurant all the time,' Alice cried. 'He makes those sorts of arrangements.'

James stroked her hair gently. 'Don't be silly,' he said. 'Pimps don't sit around in restaurants. I'm just trying to explain about Porter. He's virile in body as well as mind and he's brilliant, Alice. Everyone listens when he talks. I wish you could understand. Five thousand people applauded him at the conference and he likes *me*.'

Alice gazed at James's ecstatic face.

'He gave me some farewell advice,' James went on, eyes brilliant. 'Never work on anything trivial, he told me. Pick the important subjects.' James stroked his beard nervously, his face full of inspiration. 'He couldn't quite say it outright but he let me know that he'd sponsor my career if I do my part. That's what I've always needed. A mentor.'

'Great,' Alice said, conscious of the uselessness of this mild, approving word, knowing she was failing James by not understanding the nature of academia. She listened carefully while James described the meal he and Professor Porter had enjoyed together in a first-class hotel.

'We'll have to be seen more,' James announced. 'God! We live like recluses. I have to be high profile. Get rid of those pathetic nobodies who hang around here.'

'But James,' Alice said, her stomach contracting with shame because she was unable to distinguish a first-rate intellectual from an impostor. 'There are qualities of soul,' she began. 'Attributes like kindness and loyalty are important. Take Gordon, for example.' She knew her statements sounded foolish and weak, the words of a nobody.

'Gordon would be loyal to a dead rat,' James snapped. 'Intellectually he's mediocre or less. Grow up, Alice. There are people who matter and others who don't. I'm sorry, but that's the way it is and I've wasted too much time on the latter category.'

Alice listened to the sounds of traffic in the street. James was a deeply sensitive human being, Alice reasoned, frightened by her own inability to comprehend his new point of view, by the way his ideas seemed banal and even cruel. His integrity was fierce, his mind elegant and noble; therefore, it followed that she had some vast defect in her understanding.

'James wants to take me to the symphony,' she confided later to Michael. 'But I'm supposed to find the right outfit. He says I don't have anything appropriate. What exactly do women wear to the Queen Elizabeth Theatre?'

'Those unconventional intellectuals,' Michael commented nastily.

'Tell me,' she begged.

'Look. I'll take you to a Sunday afternoon concert. You can do your own research.'

'Do you mind?' Alice asked James later that evening.

He was silent for a moment, preoccupied. 'No,' he said, finally. 'I was just thinking how well it would work out because I've got to go home for Sunday dinner with my parents.' He turned away from Alice as he spoke. When they went to bed she lay against the hard, thin pillow while James slept beside her, blowing air out of his mouth in soft puffs of sound. Outside everything was wet with winter rain that fell through the streetlamp's desolate circle of illumination. Alice turned fretfully, catching her foot in the rip in the bottom of the sheet, torn by James's toenails which he refused to cut himself. She often performed the task for him, lifting his pale, passive foot and clipping the thick nails with her sewing scissors.

In the dark theatre with Michael, Alice watched as musicians playing various instruments created sounds she'd formerly heard as fused, emitted by a radio or a record. The great sweeping ascent of Beethoven's Pastoral Symphony caught her up and she knew her concerns were trivial compared to the vastness and glory of the music. Though she was aware of Michael watching her, she didn't turn her head. When the concert was over he took her hand and held it to his mouth while she gazed at his face, certain the only way life could be borne was to realize the human soul could create perfection.

She reported these ideas to James who exclaimed, 'The Pastoral Symphony! That old warhorse!'

'There were people playing violins of different sizes,' she added. 'Some quite large.'

'Violas, violas!' James corrected, clapping his hand to his forehead.

Alice ignored his words, describing how the theatre had darkened except for the glowing stage and then sound flooded the hall with splendour.

CHAPTER TWENTY-FOUR

So it'd been Phillipa all along, not Mara.

Alice gazed through the window of the Skillet Café and watched as James stretched his arms across a table towards Phillipa, his face intent. During the break between her split shift Alice had dashed to Raymond Your Hair Stylist where Mr Raymond himself had cut her hair which now fell forward in two curves from which her face peeked out whitely. Couldn't the expression on James's face simply reflect the love for Alice he was describing to Phillipa? Alice wondered desperately as the pair stepped out on to the sidewalk. The restaurant door swung shut behind them and Phillipa whirled in a spirited movement while James caught at her.

Alice turned at the corner of Robson and Granville, moving carefully like an old woman. The cruel faces she passed were triumphant as if transfixed by memories of their former betrayals of the weak and credulous. Afternoon light fell in long, threatening blades across the street and she hid in the shadowed lane beside Rivers' Restaurant, remembering how she'd drifted foolishly into James's world like someone in a dream, barely conscious. Now she ground her teeth in frustration and rage, sobbing beneath the fan rattling in an air conditioning vent.

'I know I shouldn't be upset,' Alice cried to Michael on the pay phone at the corner. 'It's nothing compared with problems like world famine,' she wept. 'I was the one who pushed my way into James's life. What else could he do? I was standing there with those cardboard cartons.'

'I think he had a few other options,' she heard Michael say reasonably.

She'd stood in James's kitchen like a refugee. How pathetic, she thought now, gripping the telephone receiver and forcing herself not to crawl weeping and sobbing out of the phone booth.

'James has told me before that I've been infected by bourgeois notions of conduct between men and women,' she admitted. 'Emotion is useless and wrong if it's based on shoddy, unexamined ideas, don't you think?'

'No,' Michael growled.

Alice returned despondently to the dark restaurant where Nikos wagged an admonitory finger at her for being late and Leo gave her a sour look. She saw all the tables were filled with happy people laughing before going home to have sex and love. Maybe her mother was right and only extreme deviousness was appropriate in a world populated by liars.

'I wanted to be in formless, endless connection with you,' James said bitterly when she confronted him in the bedroom that night. They could hear Gordon making tea in the kitchen. 'Now you turn it into something base and common.'

'I am common,' Alice wailed, yanking out a chair so its legs screeched across the floor. She sat and stared coldly at him while he lay on the bed with his arms folded under his head.

'You're not,' James answered. 'That's why I picked you, for God's sake. It was heart-breaking to see you in that classroom. You shone in that room. You drew me to you. It was over with Phillipa months ago but I didn't tell you about it because I didn't want to hurt you.'

Alice repeated his statement to herself, feeling the word 'over' opening her heart again.

'I saw her walking along Granville and we had coffee.'

'You put your arms around her,' Alice said stubbornly.

'I can't believe this,' James cried. 'So what?'

Although she flinched he took her limp arms and placed them around him, patting her back comfortingly as if she were a child. 'You have to trust me,' he crooned. 'You're the most important person in the world to me. I love you.'

Soothed by these incantatory phrases, Alice allowed herself to be led over to James's bed where she lay awake for a long time, staring into the darkness while James's arm lay warm across her chest. She felt she was falling, a long process in which she tumbled through dark space in a dizzy descent. This falling was love, she supposed. James was right, she'd been guilty of mentalism, living in her mind, which would doom her to the limitation of the mundane.

James was very tender towards her until a couple of evenings later when he reported that Beryl had telephoned his mother, talking for over an hour and detailing the perversions her daughter had been led into by James. 'It was quite frightening,' James cried. 'Your family is starting to affect me, Alice. I'm sorry, but I'm not a saint. I can't take much more of this.'

'I thought you said my mother was in some kind of struggle with me for sexual power.'

'I don't care about all that!' James shouted, jumping up. 'I just want peace so I can do my work and have a life.'

Alice sat numbly at the table. Wasn't James a bohemian? How could a bohemian have a normal life and why would he want one? In the bathroom she pulled on a flannel nightgown that used to be fresh and bright. All the cheap little shifts and dark sweaters she'd found on the bargain table at the Army and Navy had stretched or shrunk, were matted or hanging with frayed threads. When she walked through the kitchen to the bedroom, James was leaning in a corner, tense, as if at a word or touch he'd whirl like an animal. In her mind she held an image of James's open mouth, lips pulled back over a small arch of teeth.

She crawled into bed, arranging the pillow carefully because if there were creases in it she knew she wouldn't be able to sleep. Placing her hot cheek on the edge of the pillowcase she kept the curve of the pillow under her temple. In the kitchen she could hear the kettle boiling. Now James would walk over to the cupboard where the tea was kept. He would hesitate for a moment, perhaps forgetting his purpose. Then he'd glance at the kettle and recall he wanted the box of teabags. The pain in Alice's chest was like a fist closing around her ribs.

The next day she was really ill and Nikos sent her home from work. Wrapped in blankets she sat at the kitchen table drinking lemon and honey then dragged herself into bed. When James returned from the university he stood and stared down at her.

'I've got the killer 'flu,' she whispered. .

James found an old sleeping-bag and placed it on the floor next to the bookshelf. 'I'll let you get some rest,' he said as he leaned his head against the leg of his desk, his neck at right angles to his body. In this position he held up a review article.

After a while he sighed, switched off the light and lay flat, folding his hands across his chest and gazing at the ceiling. Alice pushed herself up from bed and crept into the kitchen. His thesis committee was arguing about his last chapter, the one that drew all his arguments together. Two committee members were on one side of the argument while the committee chairman was on the other. James said they were trying to destroy his manhood. A committee was an unnatural invention, he told Alice, because it was composed of rivals competing for the true prize of academic endeavour: sex.

The next morning James announced he had a lunch meeting in the faculty club at the university and Alice waved goodbye from her heap of blankets. James was beginning to get job offers from English Departments across the country and even from the US, but these were tentative and verbal. This was a bad time for Alice to get sick, he said.

'Don't worry,' she assured him, coughing.

Gordon had already left for work, pounding down the dusty stairs in new, stiff brogues. In a way it was a kind of pleasure to have a high temperature, Alice thought when she was alone. The leaves on the dead plant were silver in the light and she laid her hand on the cool, dark plastic of the radio. When Gordon stamped back up the stairs in the afternoon he bought chicken soup from the Hong Kong Kitchen. James was late because he had to go out for drinks with members of the department and then to dinner at the head of the department's house. Afterwards he paced back and forth while he described the evening to Alice and Gordon, his anxious fingers smoothing the edge of his tweed jacket. Professor Porter had given a brilliant talk at the university and James was full of recollection. All Porter's friends were famous and his conversation was peppered with the names of the illustrious. 'The people who've really done something!' James cried, eyes fervent. W. H. Auden! Stravinsky! While travelling in France, Porter had spent an afternoon with Cocteau! Alice bent over like an old woman and ran hot water so she could breathe in clouds of vapour. Under her bare feet the floor was icy.

CHAPTER TWENTY-FIVE

'GOLDIE'S PASSED AWAY. He was a good, clean man but now he's gone,' Beryl shrieked. She'd telephoned in the morning after the men had left.

'When?' Alice gasped, crouching on the floor beside the telephone, staring at her hands which were as white and limp and useless as gloves on the black receiver.

'Yesterday. No. The night before that,' Beryl yelled. 'Maggie's been here because I couldn't be alone. I've been through hell. He shoulda been in a nursing home. I thought I might have a heart attack when he started wheezing and turning blue right in front of me. When the ambulance came, Goldie says, "Do you mind sitting me up a bit, son. I'm having trouble catching my breath," and this nice-looking ambulance man, very polite, rolls up the back of the stretcher.

'He died in the ambulance,' Beryl continued. 'They asked me if I wanted to go with him but I'm not driving all over the city with a corpse. Anyways, I had David snivelling in the hall. He broods, you know. My nerves are shot, Maggie says.'

Alice put her hand over the receiver so her mother wouldn't hear the strange sounds coming from her mouth.

'David will be taken care of, Ben says.'

'When is the funeral?' Alice whispered. Her hair was stuck to her face.

'Oh, that's long past,' Beryl answered in a superior voice. 'Don't you know anything? Jews have the funeral right away. He's already buried.'

'I would have gone,' Alice wailed.

'You?' Beryl screamed. 'What were you to Goldie?'

*

Michael spoke very carefully, as if Alice might have difficulty understanding him. 'I'm going to pick you up,' he told her. 'Watch for my car. It's dark blue.'

'You have a car?' she echoed, coughing. She put down the receiver with hands that were dry and hot, her mind charged with images of Mr Goldman in a box beneath the earth.

She had pneumonia, the young doctor at the hospital told her when he handed her the prescription. She sat on the edge of the gurney in the emergency ward, dangling her feet while he demanded to know why she hadn't seen a doctor until now. She forced herself to answer, resisting the weakness that made her want to fall back on to the stiff, white hospital sheets. Finally, the doctor flicked the curtain closed and strode to the waiting-room to talk to Michael.

Alice took off the thin, green gown and dropped it on the pillow where it lay in a crumpled shape like frozen waves. She could hear bells and the whisper of an occasional voice on the intercom as she drew on her black tights. Weakness and hopelessness overwhelmed her when she noticed bits of lint against the black. The world was so full of imperfection! On the wall a thermometer soaked in a vial of cold alcohol and a rubbery blood-pressure apparatus was hooked to a rectangular gauge. Alice slid her feet into her black suede shoes that were loose and stretched from being soaked in rain, and as she walked across the white floor with its faint speckles she felt as if she were skating slowly towards Michael, her legs moving back and forth in long motions, like flying. Outside needles of rain fell on her skin and she climbed gladly into Michael's car. The sound of the rain was very loud and Alice had trouble hearing what Michael was saying. Water ran down the car windows in tiny rivulets.

'I'm going to take care of you,' Michael told her. 'You'll stay in my spare bedroom.' She lay back against the seat, too exhausted to argue. Her chest was hot, burning with pain that seeped into her shoulders and neck. While she waited in the car for Michael who was picking up her prescription, she watched a blinking sign pulsing in time to the pain behind her left eye. Why hadn't the doctor liked her, she puzzled, almost weeping.

She slid into cool sheets in Michael's high bed, whimpering at the touch of the bedclothes on her skin and the coldness of the water he gave her to drink with the orange pill. Then she awakened to something hissing in the dark.

'Vaporizer,' Michael's voice said soothingly when she looked around in panic.

'I'm not good,' she cried in a high voice. 'All my conversations with Mr Goldman were imaginary.' She pressed her hot face into Michael's cool shoulder, feeling the sinews standing out. 'I'm cursed,' she said in a thin, hysterical voice, panting with need to make Michael understand.

Dim morning light shone around the margins of the blind when she awoke. 'I called and cancelled my classes today,' Michael said. 'Relax, okay? I'm going to be here.' Alice smiled politely to reassure him but she knew she didn't need him there at all. She leant over the edge of the bed in a spasm of coughing while Michael thumped her back, explaining the doctor had told him to do this. When he brought her a tray set with blue crockery she picked at the eggs and drank the apple juice. Michael snapped up the blind and sat by the window reading a newspaper. 'I called your room-mates,' Michael said. 'So they know where you are.' She drifted into a feverish, half-awake state as she listened to Michael turning pages and the rain flooding over the gutters, splashing on to the ground. Her body radiated heat.

Michael bought her a popsicle in the late afternoon and she sucked the frozen shape, feeling anaesthetic coldness trickling down her throat. He insisted she consume large quantities of liquids because the doctor had given these instructions.

'They always say that,' she complained.

'So? Do you want novelty?' Michael teased awkwardly as he set a jug of water and a glass beside the bed. 'Are you suffering from ennui as well as pneumonia?'

Alice awakened in the night and wandered around Michael's house in the dark with Riley, the cat, rubbing at her ankles. Her body felt light and airy, as though she might float up like an angel. She was wearing a T-shirt of Michael's and she pulled back the curtains and looked out at the shadowed houses that lined the street and the large, bare tree in the front yard. In the morning Michael brought her porridge and toast on a tray. He was dressed in a suit and his face was rested and freshly shaved.

'You look very grand,' Alice remarked.

'I can't leave my students completely ignorant of history,' he said.

Alice slept until she heard his key in the lock and the swish of wheels on the living-room floor. She saw droplets of water sparkling on the dark wool of his suit when he came into the bedroom.

'I should have been rich,' she remarked dreamily, as she ate the grapes he brought, plucking the purple fruit from thin stems and imagining herself under a thick, hot sky like chalk, in a country filled with heat and poetry. She listened as Michael told her he'd been teaching his class about how inequality was structured into society, condemning some and blessing others according to arbitrary conditions, unrelated to worth or talent. But not me, Alice thought as she pictured herself soaring above such constrictions, borne up by literature.

'Politics are so depressing,' she sighed. 'The opposite of literature.'

'Plato said poets were liars,' Michael teased. 'Literature isn't as transformative as you seem to believe.'

Alice shrugged away Plato's distant and irrelevant opinion. 'I'm well enough to go back to James,' she announced happily as Riley leapt on to the bed and sniffed delicately at the grapes.

'Strong enough for chaos?'

'It's not that bad,' Alice answered. Michael had odd ideas, possibly because he'd gained a negative impression from her own subjective reporting. Michael didn't realize she'd left out just about everything about James, his tender child's soul and his vital maleness.

That night James called and talked to her. 'I've been so worried,' he said and she pictured him gripping the receiver and frowning tensely. When he told her he was always thinking about her she felt the power of his words travel through her bloodstream like a drug. Michael drove her home the next day. Lights and signs hung everywhere while throngs of drab figures stood at street corners or moved ceaselessly along sidewalks. Wet, shining cars, their windshield wipers moving back and forth hypnotically, proceeded along Robson slowly, stopping at lights and crosswalks. When they pulled up, James was waiting just as arranged and he leaned through the driver's window and thanked Michael.

'You've made the bed,' she cried when they reached the bedroom, touched by the way James had turned down the greyish sheet at the corner. Shyly, they lay beside each other and she rubbed James's back and stroked his hair. The room smelled musty and sour, but James said she was lovely. Even his work meant nothing to him when she was away, he told her.

In bed that night Alice curled up and faced the wall, waiting for sleep. Then she heard the loud engine of a bus, its wheezy cessation and predictable acceleration at the nearest stop on Robson. Her body tensed, waiting for the sound of the next vehicle and she tried to conduct her breathing with metronomic regularity, but noticed she could still hear her own heart beating. She pressed her face into the feather pillow, thinking of dead chickens. When Alice was a child Beryl used to clean fowl theatrically, shrieking as she dragged offal from a bird's interior and slapping its sides in punishment for containing such disgusting organs.

James threw one of his arms over her and she lifted it off. 'What's the matter?' he said. Sometimes he tried to talk to her in the night. He had the habit of waking up for brief discussions, then falling deeply into a snoring sleep like a coma. Alice lay back in misery, hearing the traffic becoming heavier as people began to leave for work. What if she never slept again? She'd read about such things: people who stopped sleeping or who hiccuped for seven years. Yet after James left she closed her eyes, dreaming she was climbing a high mountain. When she reached the summit there was an old Jewish man reading an ancient book. From each golden Hebrew letter flowed holy words that created the world.

In the afternoon James and Gordon made her tea and presented it proudly on a tray covered with crumbs. Later she heard James boasting to Gordon about her exploits. 'What does she do when she gets sick? She goes to a man in a wheelchair,' James exclaimed. 'She won't show her weakness to a whole man.' His voice was loving and admiring, as though Alice were an adorable, neurotic rebel.

CHAPTER TWENTY-SIX

WHEN SHE WENT back to work, Nikos fussed over Alice and made her eat Greek dishes that were not on the menu, standing over her as she obediently forked food into her mouth and nodded reassuringly up at him. While she'd been sick Nikos and Leo had hired a singer who came on weekends and swayed back and forth to the music of a guitar, while he sang emotional songs begging for kisses and embraces. James and Gordon both collapsed in laughter when they saw the new entertainment and had to wait for Alice outside the restaurant, but business picked up and there were lineups at the door on Saturday nights.

Alice was surprised to hear Don's voice early one morning when she staggered sleepily into the kitchen and lifted the ringing telephone; through the open door of Gordon's room she glimpsed his new suits hanging from the ornate chandelier on the ceiling. Wendy had given birth to a boy, 'Seven pounds, five ounces,' Don cried.

At the hospital Alice discovered Wendy lying beside a table covered with flower arrangements in a large ward. Wendy confided that her breasts were bandaged tightly to prevent milk forming in the glands. A pregnant woman walked by pushing a metal pole on wheels. 'She's being induced,' Wendy said.

'The husbands all look guilty,' Alice whispered back. The woman with the intravenous drip stared out the window at the end of the hall.

Wendy said she wasn't going to work until Eric was in school and Alice realized this must be the name of the baby. Then Don arrived and kissed Wendy while Alice turned and regarded the row of beds, each one containing a woman in some stage of parturition. They traipsed down the hall to the nursery window where they peered at a baby whose delicate eyelids were closed even though his tiny mouth sucked hopefully.

'Greedy,' Don said.

Wendy giggled and clasped Don's hand. 'Like his dad,' she said, smiling with peaceful, intimate pleasure. They walked Alice to the elevator when she left and stood clasped together, waving from the luminous, settled, marital planet on which they turned as the elevator doors slid shut and Alice descended to the lobby.

Beryl called the restaurant to say she'd adopted a stray cat and at night obtained perfectly good food to feed this animal from the garbage behind Safeway. 'I'm not buying stuff out of a tin,' she raged. 'Ben's not giving us that much to live on. He's the executor of Goldie's will and you can bet he watches every cent. He goes on about David's education,' she complained. 'Goldie sure had big ideas.'

'Remember how Mr Goldman and I always used to decorate the Christmas tree?' Alice asked. She turned and saw Michael come through the restaurant's front door. Mr Goldman had always asked her opinion about the placement of each bulb and had hung shining ornaments on the stiff branches despite religious differences. 'Wasn't he kind?' she exclaimed, waving at Michael. 'Wasn't he broad-minded?'

'I can't remember everything,' Beryl said irritably. 'So he hung up a few ornaments. Big deal!'

Alice poured Michael a cup of coffee. She didn't have to start work for a few minutes and the restaurant wasn't busy. The waitress on afternoons had already filled the containers and poured glasses of water that were stacked on the service counter. Alice took the chair opposite Michael, thinking he always looked so nice and fresh. Mr Goldman had been like that too, always fragrant of clean laundry.

She told him James had finished his thesis and his oral defence was scheduled in a week. 'The whole thing with Phillipa is in the past,' she added placidly.

Michael looked down at his cup and stirred the coffee into a tiny vortex.

'Guess what I'm doing, Michael?' Alice asked. 'I'm learning to read non-fiction. James said I'm totally undisciplined so now I read non-fiction every day for two hours.'

'Listen to this,' she called out to James that night as she followed him through the flat, reading aloud. 'Lawrence almost kicked a dog to death! How could he?' In Lawrence's essays she was startled to find many of James's ideas. James groaned but he allowed her to read to him while he soaked in his bath, surrounded by piney suds. Alice thought it was just like being married, not a conventional, merely legal union, but the tender, daily intimacy of mated souls.

'You looked through my desk?' James screamed.

In the morning, Alice made herself read a certain quota of non-fiction which was serious and required dedication, but without the fictional dream she found her attention moving to the untidy piles of papers on James's desk, worried his preoccupations were so unlike her own. When he told her about the professor who had not been given a merit increment for several years; the secretary who stayed late in the office hoping some professor would ask her out to dinner; the recent complaint by a family from Kamloops that their eighteen year old was receiving passionate letters from her teacher, Alice was conscious of the inadequacy of her response. He described the activities of beings so foreign she couldn't judge what kinds of acts were normal and which indicated startling or even dangerous lapses. She plucked the carbon copy of a letter written by James to Porter from a pile of other papers. The letter was obviously an answer to one by Porter offering James a year of postdoctoral study at McGill, and James had accepted the offer, promising to arrive in Montreal in January.

'If I didn't tell you,' James said through stiff lips, 'it's because I didn't want a scene like this one.' He jumped out of bed and pulled on his clothes with his back towards Alice.

'The letter was dated September.'

'I don't need this, Alice,' James said harshly. 'I'm under a great deal of pressure to perform.'

'Don't you want me to go with you?' she asked.

'There are difficulties,' James said, his dark eyes glancing away from her. 'We can't go on pretending they aren't there. I know you're terribly worried too.'

'Problems?' Alice repeated, amazed. Was that all it was? He still loved her. 'I don't know what they are,' she said touching his arm. 'Really, I don't.'

James sighed and pulled away. 'I know that's not true,' he said. 'I'm sure you're just as concerned as I am about our different backgrounds.'

'But you said my background made me more interesting,' Alice said, puzzled.

'I'm sorry,' James shrieked, punching the wall. Bits of plaster crumbled and fell on the bookcase in chalky pieces. 'I have to go,' he sobbed. 'You must see it's impossible.'

Alice rocked back and forth on the edge of the bed, trying to grasp the concepts James was presenting. He was acting as if his life was arranged by somebody else, Professor Porter maybe. What if James had some terrible difficulty with logical thought? He must see she could go with him to Montreal where they could be happy, walking through snow. 'Do you think that I couldn't get a job in Montreal?' she asked.

This produced fresh sobs from James, whose thin chest heaved while his mouth opened in a howl of weeping. 'You don't understand,' he cried, smacking his fist against the wall again.

'I could get a waitress job in a couple of days,' Alice said. 'We could take separate apartments in the same building or something. Is that the problem? You don't want Professor Porter to know you're living with a woman. Is that it?'

'I'm sorry,' James wept. 'I'm sorry.'

'So you don't want me,' Alice whispered.

'I do,' he cried, reaching towards her and sobbing into her neck. 'You're very precious to me. Always remember that.'

Alice sat stiffly, waiting for his sobs to finish, her neck wet with his tears. She reasoned wildly, unable to understand what James meant because he had said they were perfectly balanced in their relationship which was heroic, in a way, deeper and more honest than the unions of those who respected societal forms. He was quiet now and began to unbutton her nightdress.

She shouted and jumped up, amazed at the loudness of her voice.

'Look,' James's voice was reasonable and controlled. 'You're over-reacting.'

'You fraud,' Alice said, breathing painfully. 'Talk about *mauvaise foi*.'

'Jesus,' James said. '*Mauvaise foi*. Where did you learn that? Woolworth's? You don't know what you're talking about for God's sake.'

'I had to meet people of your class to discover the true meaning of bad faith,' Alice retorted, sobbing and pulling out a dresser drawer in a sharp movement so it stuck at an angle. In place of her reading regime, her candlelit bohemian dinner parties, her future with James and all its campuses, coffee shops, books, music, the great wonder of art opening to her in unending revelation, she could feel nasty diminishing bitterness growing in her, killing her soul. 'I'm not tough enough to be with people like you,' she panted. 'Liar! Betrayer!'

She snatched her clothes from the drawer and knelt on the floor folding and refolding them. 'Finally we have the truth,' she said while her fingers rapidly did up buttons and smoothed faded cloth. 'Now I find out what you really think of me.'

James crouched on the floor beside her, trying to peer into her face but she kept her head down. 'Look at me,' he pleaded, reaching for her hand. 'You're not thinking rationally.'

'Who cares?' Alice sobbed. 'You're the one who said you despised the primacy of the rational.'

'I let you believe what you wanted to believe, maybe,' James said truculently, his hair hanging forward. 'But let's not forget your part in it. I came to the conclusion a long time ago that I couldn't take you with me. Be realistic, for once. You work in a restaurant. I'm going to be a professor.' He sighed. 'I don't know how to put it more clearly.'

'I do,' Alice said, stuffing her collection of D. H. Lawrence books into a shopping bag and covering them with clothing.

The phone rang and James answered it. 'She's busy right

now,' he said, putting down the receiver. 'You see?' he said to Alice when he walked back into the bedroom. 'That was your mother. Her cat's disappeared or something.' He shook his head. 'Do you think I'm going to put up with that kind of thing for the rest of my life?'

'You should have told me the truth,' Alice insisted. She was dressed now and stood with her shopping bag and purse ready. 'You kept me by lying.'

'The truth,' James said with contempt. 'I'm not going to be trapped, Alice. Especially by someone else's conception of the truth.'

Call me back, she thought, walking to the door, the heavy bag in her hand.

'This isn't the end,' James said helplessly.

Alice wrenched open the door and ran clumsily down the dark tunnel of the staircase and out into the rainy street where she strode off as though certain of her intended direction. She wished she could dash to some bar frequented by criminals and assassins and plunge into adventure. The bag in her hand grew damp and water ran down her face and arms but she welcomed the deluge. James was right, she grieved. She was a dreamer, swooning before the throne of art instead of seeing poison letters lying on desks. By abandoning her, he had shown himself to be an adult, practical and realistic. Alice imagined his parents offering secret advice.

Dizzy with revelation, she stared into a store window filled with painted canisters of tea and coffee. Why had she never even seen James's parents' house, she thought frantically. She recalled with pain she had never looked at James's office or his department at the university. Had James feared her presence the way she was terrified of Beryl's appearance? James might have dreaded her mouth opening in laughter at the wrong moments or speaking of painfully uneducated yearnings.

Yet Alice was aware of herself waiting for the pounding of James's footsteps on the street, the sudden appearance of his reflection in the window. She wondered if he was looking for her, wandering without a jacket in the rain but searching the wrong streets. Perhaps he would say someone had influenced him to be hard, Professor Porter or his father, and now he'd come to his senses and realized she was the flesh of his flesh. She didn't really care what words he used if only he would say them. Her own reflection in the glass was absurd, a pale woman with uncombed, wet hair and stricken eyes like an animal.

It was clear everything was her fault. Although she'd sensed she was in the group of people destined to be shut out of life she'd none the less persisted. She loved James with the love of an unlovable person, holding out an awkward, burdensome offering like a bleeding organ proffered to a vegetarian. Nothing was more useless and horrifying. There was something unformed about her, perhaps even repulsive, Alice thought. She moved in a miasma of sadness and boredom which formed her natural atmosphere and when she tried to escape from this her actions and mannerisms were unnatural, easily betraying her as an interloper. James had recognized this when desire faded. It was only that which had protected her until now. Mara and Phillipa, unswayed by sexual attraction, had flashed out rays of contempt long ago.

Alice turned and trudged stolidly through the rain, coatless, her shoes spongy with water. She walked past normal, properly-dressed people while acting as though she were unconcerned by the fact that a wet shopping bag was slapping against her leg and rain was falling in wet tatters on to her olive jumper. In a huddle of people wearing raincoats she stood waiting on the sidewalk for the lights to change. She imagined James conferring with his friends, she could see they had been his friends not hers, and planning just what he should do about the problem of Alice. Shame and fear dazzled her in a blinding transport and she wondered if she'd faint in the street.

She turned off Robson Street, past a corner grocer where hard polished fruit lay in pyramids, and walked vaguely through streets where bare, unhealthy city trees held up their branches in cold, polluted air. Bleak, wooden rooming houses with derelict porches and closed net curtains suggestive of misery stood on either side of the streets amid newer, sleek apartment towers where single people led careless, stylish lives. Alice felt weary and sick. She was like an insect on a little point of land surrounded by freezing, grey water, the terrible sea featured in lying postcards.

It seemed fitting when she knocked on Michael's door that there was no answer and she had to crouch on his front porch and wait, cradling her wet things in her arms. Behind her, Michael's cat eyed the grey curtain of rain that fell around the porch, separated from the damp cold by a pane of glass. When Michael finally arrived she stood at the top of the ramp. 'I've left James,' she called out and as he turned the key in the lock she was already describing the letter, how it had been lying there and she had lifted it up slowly and read it as if in a trance, the way that girl in the fairy tale had grasped the poison apple. 'He said I'd invited his deception,' Alice gasped frantically. Everything was different now, she realized. James was carrying on with his life which had nothing to do with her and never would. 'I'm such a fool,' she cried to Michael while he set his books on the table. She dropped her damp bag by the front door. 'I thought I could do everything,' she sobbed. 'It's the liar who has all the power. Everyone despises the dupe.'

The cat leapt into Michael's lap and he drew his hand along the animal's fur, his fingers moving delicately over its head. Outside the rain continued to fall heavily, a flat, dreary downpour and the sky grew darker as Alice talked desperately in her effort to describe everything with vivid clarity so Michael's eyes would gleam with understanding. 'I thought James was full of noble ideas,' she groaned. 'An intellectual pursuing ideals.'

Michael remarked, 'I always thought he was a creep.'

Alice wanted to hear such things, statements that defined James as defective, but she knew this was the pettiness of the outcast.

Everything went on as before. The customers said exactly the same kinds of things and she responded in the same way, although her voice was tense.

'That nosy parker from next door did something to my cat,' Beryl raged on the restaurant phone.

'You can't be sure,' Alice said carefully.

'Of course, you'd say that because you don't give a shit,' Beryl snapped. 'Anyways, I paid her back. She won't be seeing her cat again. I made sure of that. When I figured out what she did I bought some poison.'

Alice interrupted but Beryl raised her voice, describing how she'd enticed the neighbour's cat over at midnight and shut it in the kitchen with a bowl of food mixed with rat poison. 'I'm not a cruel person,' she explained to Alice. 'But justice has to be done.'

Michael waited up for Alice. He was working in his room where he'd laid a fire. It was a large room with a heavy oak desk underneath the curtained window and there was an upholstered chair beside the fireplace. She sat in it wearily with her eyes closed while she told Michael that Beryl had advanced from complaint to action. Michael handed her cocoa and she drank the liquid without tasting it, setting the empty cup on the warm hearth. 'You're good to me,' she sighed.

'I'd rather you didn't think of me as a nurse,' Michael said fiercely. 'I called your house once, you know. After you gave me your number that time in the Heidelberg. I wish you'd been in then.'

In the warm radiance, the sheen of Alice's skin under Michael's hands was delicate as he unfastened her clothes and she moved to help him. She lay on his bed languidly, watching the changing shapes of light and dark on the ceiling like images in a dream. Michael came back into the room naked in the firelight and pulled himself on to the bed in a powerful movement. The wheelchair clanked and Alice closed her eyes. 'Hear that?' Michael asked. 'Yes,' she answered nervously. 'That's the sound of my chastity belt being unlocked,' he whispered. She pressed her fingers on to the slope of his back and smiled.

Afterwards she was tranquil in the warm room. 'It was just like D. H. Lawrence,' she breathed reverently. 'Don't laugh,' she cried, slapping him when she saw his shoulders shaking. Michael snorted with suppressed mirth. Alice didn't understand how the body could want life even when consciousness was exhausted and defeated. She stretched out in Michael's bed while flames in the fireplace cast flowing light into the room.

CHAPTER TWENTY-SEVEN

WHEN ALICE AWAKENED she was aware she had to endure the rest of her life without James. The realization formed while she slept and she knew that even when she'd been running through the rain all her senses had been alert to James's continued presence in her life. She'd developed a self that was like James, that told stories about work like someone issuing flashy bulletins from an interesting, amusing world, but this superior, literary point of view had faded. Alice regarded her white feet with their thin blue veins as typical of a waitress, feet that would spread and swell as the years went on, delicate veins twisting into purplish ropes. James and his friends, with their educated, drawling comments, had rescued her from the inevitability of banal suffering. Now she'd been dropped, she'd fallen into a familiar domain of terror and hopelessness. All she could do was silently endure her fate. She was not like James and his friends. Of course Michael would try to tell her she was superior to James's crowd in some useless spiritual way, but she would not be comforted by that because she knew it was not true.

In the fireplace soft, grey ash and bits of charred wood were left from the warm flames of the previous evening. She remembered Michael's intent, alert face and the deep tenderness that flowed from him, sweeping her into its ecstatic flood. Even now she regretted not reaching out for him in the morning when she'd sensed him watching her before he left. When the telephone rang she knew at once it would be Beryl but she thought that if it was not, if it was Michael, or James, or a stranger, or even a wrong number, the call might be a sign that she could have a remarkable life after all. Alice made her way to the black plastic instrument slowly.

'I got your number from that James weirdo,' Beryl snarled when Alice answered. 'Jeez, you're living with another one, now? Are they lined up at the door, or what?' Her bitter, nasal voice went on to say Alice had to take a bus over to North Vancouver right away because upon her doctor's advice she was checking herself into the hospital to recover from stress and depression.

'How long are you going into the hospital?'

'As long as it takes,' Beryl cried vindictively. 'It's worry over you that's done all this to me.'

Alice wrote a note for Michael on a pad of lined paper with handwriting that was so chaotic she ripped up a couple of attempts and stuffed the pieces of paper into her purse. The call to Nikos was more difficult, but he finally told her to go ahead and agreed to give her the early shift beginning the following day.

On the long bus ride to North Vancouver, Alice noticed images of Michael surfacing in her mind, even though she told herself sternly that romantic notions were foolish, inappropriate and even dangerous. All the lovely tenderness of the night before was incomprehensible to her. Michael was her friend! It startled her that someone in this neutral, comfortable category could be transformed into a lover. Everything had seemed so inevitable, she admitted to herself with a kind of shocked delight, but she didn't know what it all meant. She was still trying to sort things out when the bus turned on to Lonsdale Avenue.

As soon as Alice reached her mother's house, Beryl slapped down the path in her thongs while she shouted instructions to Alice. With a cigarette hanging from her mouth, Beryl yanked open the door of the taxi and climbed in, a small figure in the corner of the back seat, jiggling with the vehicle's motion as it drove off.

Alice entered the silence and dereliction of the house, shutting the door behind her and wandering through rooms filled with a sharp stench. The state of the house was worse than it had been. She located dried faecal pools, probably from the vanished cat. These she scraped off with a knife, sweeping the shreds of filth into a dustpan and scrubbing at the stained patches on the floor with a gritty cleanser that burned her fingers.

The place was cold and damp, with blotches of greeny-black mould growing along the baseboards and blossoming up the outside walls of the living room, where each surface was covered with filthy dishes and cups, some containing additional colonies of mould. There were wormlike burn marks on the table beside Beryl's chair and on the carpet nearby. Alice had an impression of great darkness and heaviness in the room even though it was only two o'clock. When she unscrewed the greyish globes in the lamp she heard the faint sound of broken filaments.

In the kitchen, a corner of the table had been cleared and covered with a newspaper where David's bowl from breakfast stood beside a crust soaked in mustard. The refrigerator was empty except for plastic bags and greenish liquid in the crisper. There were so many dishes and pots piled on the counters Alice suspected Beryl of buying new crockery at the Salvation Army instead of washing the dishes she already owned.

When David came in he found her pouring boiling water into the sink and she regarded the child through a cloud of steam, imagining, in place of the squalor, a warm, orderly house where objects fell into categories that did not overlap and could therefore be stored rationally. All these dishes were in different shapes and patterns so even after she'd washed them she wasn't sure how they should be arranged. Standing in the cold dampness, Alice realized that her discouragement and fatigue had put a stop to her musings about the night that had just passed. This was just as well, she told herself, because only a superficial person would move from one man to the next as though they were interchangeable. Nevertheless, the perfect, still images of herself and Michael in the warm room remained with her and she could gaze at them as if they were clear and detailed photographs.

She pried dried material from plates and dropped them into soapy water, pushing as many as possible underneath concealing suds. Her body cringed from the cold while David sat at the table with his jacket on, watching her cautiously. When the hot water was finished she stacked the rest of the crockery and made herself walk through the trailing, wet grass in the back yard to peer at the murky gauge in the oil tank. The red needle pointed near the bottom.

While they waited for the water to heat again, she told David they would go to a park, and later the child led her to a small playground. She sat on a damp seat in the corner of a sandbox, while he clambered over metal monkey bars or soared back and forth on a swing. Although her body was stony, heavy with desolation, she roused her will and forced herself to wave encouragingly at him. She could not think of one household task that could ever be satisfactorily accomplished. Only miraculous transformation could restore the sloping, uneven kitchen floor with its worn linoleum, black and curled at the edges. David came running over to her like a puppy, gazing up with his dark eyes squeezed into crescent shapes by his smile. She took his hand in hers and he trotted quietly at her side as they walked towards Lonsdale Avenue.

'We're going out for dinner,' Alice announced. 'Won't that be fun?'

In the café he wolfed his food while she worried about the problem of his school lunch. David was utterly helpless and totally dependent on her, she realized. She watched him as he spooned ice-cream into a mouth smeared with the remnants of his dinner.

'Do you know your Uncle Ben's last name?' she asked.

'Who?' David looked alarmed at her question.

'Never mind,' she said.

While he'd played she'd worried about his evening meal and now that he was eating it she moved on to concern over his bedtime wash. She imagined there was a good chance soap would have to be purchased. Each activity she considered was composed of small details and failure was possible at each step. At the moment, David's hair looked long and dirty, his neck ringed with grime. When he'd stood next to her in the playground she'd noticed a dusty odour, like a room that had been shut up and neglected. The front of his flannel shirt was stiff with slops, the bottom stuffed into corduroy trousers stained green at the knees. He wore no socks.

'I don't like that white cheese,' David whispered at the corner store, so she placed the pale rectangle back in the cooler and selected orange cheddar instead. On the counter next to the cash register she placed bread, soap and waxed paper and while the man counted up the total she added a package of baseball cards. The small, dim store was pungent with a metallic, comforting scent from the inside of the metal cooler where bottles of soda pop were immersed in cold, shallow water.

David broke a sweet square of gum into pieces and stuffed them into his mouth as they left the warm store. Alice wanted to see herself as a restorer of order, a quick, competent figure who'd make beds in a flash while a nutritious mixture of meat and vegetables simmered deliciously on the stove. She must show Beryl and David such things were possible. David should be clean and fresh, dressed in ironed clothing like that of other children, his hair clipped by a barber. Then playmates would seek him out. She recalled her own dread of the school bell that signalled those occasions when other children would rush screaming into the schoolyard and she'd lean against the brick wall of the school, her hair frizzed out in a witchy explosion from one of Beryl's home permanents, her ears scabbed with hardened dirt. No child would dare give her permission to join any group.

'Do they have fingernail inspection in your school?' she asked David. She supposed he should be soaked for a long time in hot water, though she dreaded the prospect of touching the tub with its greenish stains and intimate rings.

In the bathroom, they searched for the plug and Alice discovered it in a clump of cottony dust underneath the clawed iron bathtub. David giggled when her hand reached into the dark space and closed around the circle of rubber with its bit of beaded chain still attached. She poured bleach into the tub and added hot water, leaving this germicidal solution to soak while she finished the dishes.

'This isn't harmful,' she assured David, rinsing it out later, although a bright orange stain had appeared on the bottom of the bath.

David objected to Alice washing his hair but she insisted, lathering his head while he sat in the warm, steaming water with his eyes screwed shut in alarm. From the crown of froth she scraped some bubbles and dabbed a soap beard on to his chin, holding the little mirror from her purse so he could see. He tittered with nervous delight, tipping his head back obediently so she could rinse out the soapsuds and she slopped water down her own sleeve with desperate movements in her attempt to remove every trace of shampoo without getting any in his eyes. His small body was stiff with tension. Suddenly he screamed and shot up in the tub, rubbing his eyes and thrashing while water surged over the edge of the bath.

'I'm sorry. I'm sorry,' Alice said, swishing cold water on to his face so he howled more loudly, his face twisted with pain and rage. Frantic, she lifted the child out and wrapped him in a hard, thin towel, blotting his face and rubbing at his ragged hair. She rocked him back and forth helplessly.

When his cries subsided, she carried him into the cold living room and set him on the couch, tucking a grey army blanket around him. He seemed soothed by the television when she turned it on, his large eyes fixing at once on the moving, familiar images.

Tangled in a heap of clean laundry tossed on her old bed, Alice found several pyjama tops but bottoms were more difficult to locate. She knelt in front of David's dresser, forcing herself to take out garments methodically and put them in neat piles. Among the knotted snarls she discovered a faded pair of pyjamas patterned with cartoon rabbits, and then turned her attention to his bed. There was a flattened piece of torn gold paper under the pillow, an old wrapping from one of Mr Goldman's cigars. She examined David's damp, striped mattress that was marked with successive patterns of stain.

'Want to sleep in my bed?' Alice asked David. Even though she could see herself making cocoa, tucking a hot-water bottle at his feet and reading him a story, she also imagined the weary, complicated search for cocoa, sugar, the hot-water bottle, its plug and a children's book. So instead she folded the sheets in a pleat beneath David's face, kissed him and turned off the light in her old room.

Afterwards, she opened Beryl's bedroom door reluctantly; she hated the idea of touching the same sheets and pillowcases Beryl had pressed her body against. The bed appeared very large, covered with clothing. There was even an old fur coat Alice had never seen before, and the close air was thick with her mother's smell. As Alice yanked back the sheet an odour of vinegar and sweat rushed up from the mattress. Deploring her own weakness, she swept the coat off the bed and pulled it over her on the couch in the living room.

When David came dancing down the hall, electric with excitement, his appearance reminded her of the tub still full of cold dirty water and the school lunch that had to be made. 'Go back to bed,' she called out and he dashed to his room.

How gracefully and lightheartedly James would explain her absence, Alice thought, remembering his resonant voice and the pleasure of his fluid, cultivated language. She breathed in loss and humiliation like fire.

There was still the library, she reminded herself, and the possibility she could begin at the first letter of the alphabet, the perfect vowel containing potential sorrow along with great opening promise. She would move slowly and in order through all the volumes on the shelves, comforting herself with the consolations of literature, the mystery and splendour of words themselves and the transports and glories of art. Then the telephone rang. 'They said I was too serious so I showed them!' Beryl yelled boisterously. 'I walked right into the patients' lounge wearing black lace panties and a brassiere!'

After her mother hung up, Alice sat on the edge of the couch and stared at the desolate, silent room but David interrupted, again appearing in the doorway, leaping with delicate, whispering movements in his bare feet, an odd, self-conscious expression on his face and his eyes gleaming with excitement and hope. Her trance disturbed, Alice turned her gaze on the child who hopped friskily in the hall while darting glances at her. He ran towards her, holding out his arms, and she jumped forward in a fury, slapping him hard across his frail shoulder. When he turned she followed him, screaming that she couldn't bear it. Sobbing, she unfastened his pyjama top and saw the red print of her hand on him with the fingers splayed out. She blotted the mark with a cool cloth. Then she put him back in bed and smoothed his hair while they regarded each other in tearless silence.

Afterwards, Alice sat alone in the cold front room. The West End seemed very distant now, glittering on a point of land that could be reached only by traversing a long bridge arched over dark water. When she remembered James's closed face and his gaze fixed on future glories, a brilliant career and clever, educated friends, she shut her eyes to stop the image. Yet even now she could feel her will rising in her. I'll survive, she thought, clenching her hands. Despite everything, she would still enter that other, vivid world of art and literature. Though hope itself might be dangerous and even sharply painful, she would not give up.

MAUREEN MOORE was born in Montreal and now lives in Vancouver.

The Illumination of Alice Mallory, her first novel, was published to critical acclaim both in Canada and in the U.K. and was shortlisted for the B.C. Book Award (The Ethel Wilson Prize).